Praise for

The Case of the Meddling Mama

What a fun read . . . Ms. Burton had me biting my nails by the end of the book. ~ Maris Soule, author of *A Killer Past*

The Case of the Bygone Brother

"...plenty of action and sexual tension that kept me turning the pages. I loved this book and these characters. I'm glad this will be a series. I can't wait until O'Hara and Palzetti are back together again." ~ Marilyn Baron, author of *Landlocked*

". . . a wonderful modern love story made sweeter with humor, family values, and Sam Spade suspense." ~ Rolynn Anderson, author of *Fear Land*

Also by Diane Burton

ROMANCE REKINDLED

A Far Haven Tale

Diane Burton

ISBN- 978-0-9990452-0-6

Dedication

To my amazing daughters, Liz and Katy

To my great sons, Doug and Matt

To my grandchildren who are growing up too fast

And especially to Bob, my best friend and hero

Acknowledgements and Thanks

To Elizabeth Carr for her invaluable advice and terrific editing. Her help made my story better. And to Florence at The Novel Difference for the amazing cover art. Thank you, ladies.

To the members of the Mid-Michigan chapter of Romance Writers of America® for their continued support and advice.

Most importantly, I want to thank my family for all their support. Liz & Matt, Doug & Katy, I'm very proud of you. Thank you for encouraging me and for giving me five delightful grandchildren.

To my husband, Bob. How glad I am that our friends fixed us up on that blind date!

Dear Reader,

Welcome to Far Haven, a small Lake Michigan resort town where everyone knows everybody's business, and home to Alex O'Hara, private investigator. I've had a lot of fun writing the series. With each book, I found characters who intrigued me. And I kept thinking they should have their story told, too. I wrote two short stories using these characters for The Roses of Prose blog's annual Christmas anthologies. Yet, in a short story, I had to write only the bare bones. I wanted to do more. Before I knew it, the *Far Haven Tales* was created.

Romance Rekindled is the first, of many, I hope, stories that take place in my fictional town of Far Haven, Michigan. You don't need to read the Alex O'Hara Novels to enjoy the *Far Haven Tales*. I hope you do, though. If you are familiar with Alex's stories, *Romance Rekindled* comes between *The Case of the Bygone Brother* and *The Case of the Fabulous Fiancé.*

My Dutch ancestors began coming to America in the 1600s. They settled in New York and New Jersey, before moving west. Some came to Michigan before it was a state. Although my ancestors didn't settle in West Michigan like many from the Netherlands, I drew on their names and others for many of my characters. In no way are these characters meant to depict any real person, living or dead. They are entirely the product of my imagination.

I hope you enjoy *Romance Rekindled.*

Diane

CHAPTER ONE

"Mom?" Bethany leaned around the corner of the living room. "I'm sorry to bail on you. I have to go to work."

Abby Ten Eyck set down the ornament she'd been about to hang on the Christmas tree in her mother's living room where it graced the front window. She wiped her hands on her jeans. Live evergreens always made her hands itchy. "I know. I appreciate all the work you and the boys have done."

She could never have hauled all the boxes down from the attic if not for the two high school boys, Bethany's friends. *Why Mother wanted them to bring down all the Christmas decorations is beyond me.*

"Grandma and I can finish up." Abby glanced at her watch. "You'd better leave now. You know how bad traffic is this weekend. Besides, you can't keep those hungry shoppers waiting."

The last place Abby wanted to be on the Sunday after Thanksgiving was at a store while the thundering horde fought for bargains. Friday and yesterday had been nightmares at her shop and would be until December twenty-fourth. Despite the increased revenue during the holidays, plus increased competition from stores in Grand Rapids, she kept to her policy of closing the shop on Sundays. Unfortunately for Bethany, the owner of the Golden Fleece Restaurant was only too willing to take advantage of the busy shoppers even on

Sundays. Nevertheless, Bethany was lucky to have a weekend job where she could earn money for college.

"This is the last box," Scott announced as he and his buddy, Todd, slowly lumbered down the stairs. "And, boy, is it heavy."

"Heavy?" Abby left the decorating and crossed the foyer to look. "Decorations aren't heavy."

At the bottom of the stairs, Scott balanced the dusty box on his knee. "Says *Christmas* on this side. It's kinda faded, though. Should we take it back up?"

His friend groaned.

Abby knew that feeling. She and Bethany had been working since after church that morning, and she was fading fast. "No. Set it in the dining room. I'll look at it later."

Bethany grabbed her jacket from the front closet, along with the boys' coats. "I can give you guys a lift if you want."

Mother bustled out of the kitchen. "Oh, dear. You aren't leaving? I made sandwiches for everybody."

Bethany hugged her grandmother. "Thanks, Gram. I'll eat at the restaurant. Gotta go. You guys coming?" She cast a glance at them.

"Sandwiches?" Scott grinned. "I'll walk home, Beth. Thanks anyway."

"Yeah. Me, too."

Both boys acted like they hadn't eaten in days. If Abby remembered correctly, her friend and mother of three teenage boys often said they were eating machines.

Mother led the boys into the kitchen while Abby hugged her daughter good-bye. "Be careful on the roads."

"Always. Love you, Mom."

As Abby responded, "Love you, too," Bethany ran out the door and down the broad front steps.

Abby closed the heavy door, not bothering to lock it. Most people in Far Haven didn't, not during the winter, anyway. Strangers rarely came to the Lake Michigan resort town when the bitter cold winds blew off the lake and cut through even the warmest coats.

At the doorway to the kitchen, Abby paused. Bethany had hung a sprig of mistletoe from the lintel. Unless her daughter brought the boy she was dating to Christmas dinner, there wouldn't be any kissing in this house. Abby had mixed feelings about Logan. He seemed nice enough, but she thought Bethany deserved someone better. Someone like Scott whom Bethany had known since grade school. Or Todd, the taciturn boy who wouldn't look Abby in the eye. Maybe not him.

When she entered the kitchen, the boys were chowing down and talking to Mother. Or rather, Scott talked. Todd just ate. Noting a luncheon plate with one sandwich set aside, she surmised it was for her.

"Thanks, Mother." As she sat, she glanced across the kitchen table at the teens who were finishing their tall glasses of milk. "You fellows did well. I can't thank you enough."

"It was nothing." Scott appeared to be the spokesperson. Todd, the quiet one, nodded.

After they finished, Abby followed them to the foyer. She handed each boy a twenty. "Thanks again."

Scott tried to give his back. "You don't need to pay us, Ms. Ten Eyck."

Belatedly, Todd did the same.

"No." She closed the boys' hands over the bills. "I want you to have it. Use it to buy your mothers a present." She grinned. "Or yourself."

Reluctantly, they stuffed the money in their jacket pockets. "Thanks," they said in unison before leaving.

At the bottom of the front steps, Todd turned around. "If you have any other work, I'd be glad to do it for you."

Abby nodded. "I'll let you know."

As they turned away, Scott elbowed his friend in the side. Before Abby closed the door, she heard him say, "That sounded like you wanted more money."

"For my mom," Todd muttered.

"Abby?" Mother called. "What is this box doing here?"

Still pondering what Todd meant, Abby turned away from the door.

Standing in the doorway to the dining room, Mother had fisted her hands on her hips. "You shouldn't have brought that down."

"Fine time to tell me, Mother. The boys just left. Besides, it says *Christmas* on the side."

Before Mother crossed the foyer into the living room, Abby thought she saw tears in her eyes.

"Mother?" Abby followed her. "What's wrong?"

Sitting in the closest chair, Mother used a tissue to wipe away a tear. Giving Abby a familiar expression, she pursed her lips. "Take that box upstairs."

Abby collapsed on the matching wingback chair. "Mother, from what the boys said that thing weighs a ton. I'm not carrying it by myself. I can't."

"Bethany can help you. Where is she?"

With a look of exasperation, Abby said, "She left for work, remember?"

"Oh. That's right." She paused for a moment. "I don't like her working in that place."

Now what? She never voiced concern before. "It's a nice restaurant. Very upscale. Great tips, according to Bethany."

"It's too far."

That it was, more than half an hour each way. Then, Abby realized what her mother had done. By focusing on Bethany, she'd moved Abby off the topic of the box in the dining room.

"Why are you upset about that box?"

Mother waved the soggy tissue. "Not important." She stood. "Time to get back to work. You can wrap the garland around the banister. You always do such a nice job with that."

Before Abby could pursue the issue of tears, Mother bustled out to the kitchen. "Don't wind that garland too tightly."

Abby gave up trying to explain anything to her mother. She didn't listen anyway. On her way to the foyer, Abby grabbed the plastic tote stuffed with the green garland they used every year since before her father passed. After six years, it might be time to invest in new. She started at the top of the stairs where it made a bend to continue up to the second floor. As she wound the silk strands around the banister and rail, she wondered about the box in the dining room. What could possibly be in it to make Mother cry?

It couldn't be something of Father's. He didn't save anything unless it pertained to his business. After his passing, his secretary had boxed up the files and put them in storage in the event that his partner in the law firm ever needed them. At home, Father tried to impose his sense of order on Mother. He never succeeded.

She wasn't a hoarder by any means. Her motto—and that of generations before her—was "we might need that someday"—evidenced by the multitude of boxes still in the attic. And furniture. All their discards, whether in good shape or not, were stored up there. One of these days, Abby would have to tackle that. She stifled a groan. Maybe in the spring.

When she finished draping the garland, she added red bows then stood back to admire her work. The greenery contrasted nicely with the white banister and rail. She grabbed the empty tote to add it to those already stacked in the dining room.

The boys had left that heavy box in the way. Using her foot, she tried to push it aside, but the weight made it move only a couple of inches on the thick beige carpet. Maybe if she took out some things it would be easier.

"What are you doing?" Mother screeched.

"I can't move the box." Abby ripped the rest of the packing tape. "I need to take out a few things, so it isn't as heavy."

"Stop right there. Do not—"

Abby pried open the lid. The box was filled to the brim with cards, letters, and journals.

Mother became a whirlwind in her rush to stop Abby from taking anything out of the box. "Just leave it. I'll deal with it later."

"It's in the way."

"All right. We'll move it together." Mother got on one side of the box, expecting Abby to comply.

"If you throw your back out—" *Or I do.* "—it will be your own fault."

Despite Mother's glaring, the two of them managed to slide the box against a wall.

"That's it, Mother. No farther."

As she stood, Mother winced then glared at Abby. "If you say, I told you so, I will . . ." She huffed. "I don't know what I'll do, but it won't be pretty. I'm going upstairs and taking a nap."

Abby looked more closely at her. Mother never took naps. Maybe trying to decorate the entire first floor had been too much for her. She did look rather pale. Pushing that box out of the way had taken more out of her than Abby expected.

"Are you all right?"

"I will be." Mother slowly climbed the stairs, taking care to step on the runner that matched the dark red oriental in the center of the foyer. At the bend, where the garland ended, she leaned against the rail. She glanced over her shoulder, chiding, "And don't you touch what's in that box."

What a quick recovery from wilting to demanding. But then that was Mother. Rapid emotion changes.

Abby pursed her lips. "I won't."

"Swear on my grave, Abigail."

Whoa. She really meant it. Abby blew out a breath. "You aren't dead yet. You don't have a grave."

"Picky, picky, picky. Swear on your father's grave."

"Mother, I said I would not look in your precious box. I have enough to do putting up the rest of the decorations you insisted the boys bring down."

Mother mounted three more steps before she looked down and said more demanding now, "On your father's grave, Abigail."

God help me. I knew coming over here was a bad idea. I should have opened the shop. But she and Bethany always helped Mother decorate for Christmas. The way this day was shaping up, Abby's temper would get the best of her. With resignation, she said, "I swear on Father's grave not to open your box."

Sheesh. You'd think she had some deep, dark secret in there.

Right. Florence Ten Eyck did not have deep, dark secrets. She'd been a proper pillar of the community for fifty years—forty-four of them while Father was alive. Though she'd changed a little lately, Mother knew her place.

Abby wished she knew hers.

Divorced women didn't have a place, as she'd discovered when she returned to Far Haven, Bethany in her arms. Her single friends wanted to bar hop, something Abby found a waste of time and money. With her married friends, she felt like a fifth wheel. Her true friends, like Alex O'Hara and Dottie Matthews, were the exceptions. Single private investigator Alex didn't bar hop, and Dottie never made Abby feel like she was intruding in her family life.

She quickly finished the ornaments on the tree. Unfortunately, each time she took a familiar one out of the box, her memory kicked in with fond thoughts of the year Bethany made or gave it to her grandmother.

Enough thinking, she chastised herself. She need to finish up and go home where another tree waited.

Two hours later, Mother came down the stairs. Her light step registered only because Abby stood in the foyer, hanging the huge wreath on the outside of the open door.

"Let me help you, dear." Mother rushed to hold the wreath while Abby hooked it in place.

"Did you have a nice nap?" Abby straightened the ribbon and anchored a wobbly pine cone.

"I tried to sleep, but too many memories raced through my mind. The wreath is a little crooked."

Abby stepped back. "You're right. Would you tip it to the right? Just a little bit."

After closing the door, Mother stood on the porch and surveyed their work. "The wreath looks fine. The girls and I had so much fun making it."

Mother's bridge group had gone to a wreath-making party the week before at a local tree farm where the owner held parties during the season. Forming tree boughs into wreaths had been more exciting to read about in the brochure than wrestling with them in real life. The one time Abby had gone, she'd come home with a wreath large enough for a barn—or the garage, which was where they'd hung it. Though Abby hadn't gone again, Mother and her friends went every year. From the size of this year's wreath, Mother had figured out the balance of boughs and size.

When they came inside, Abby said, "I'm going to take the empty boxes up to the attic."

"I'll help you." Mother bustled out to the living room.

That was a switch. She usually left the room in disarray, saying she'd tackle the mess later, which meant Abby would deal with it later.

"We have too many decorations," Mother declared after the third trip up to the attic. She surveyed the area filled with the leftovers from four generations. "When we take them down after New Year's, I want to sort them into those you and Bethie can take and those we don't want anymore."

Abby knew for sure something wasn't right. "What's wrong? Aren't you feeling well? Are the stairs too much for you?"

Mother snapped her head around. "I work out at the Senior Center three times a week. On a stairstepper, mind you, and weight machines. I'll tell you what's too much, this house." She plopped onto an old easy chair that had been Father's years ago. A cloud of dust puffed into the air.

"What do you mean? You have a cleaning service."

She waved her hand. "And a lawn and snow removal service, too. I mean, I just rattle around in this old place."

An uneasy feeling came over Abby. "You aren't thinking of selling our house, aren't you?"

Ignoring Abby's question, Mother stood and brushed her seat. "I'll get the cleaning ladies to come up here and clean. Let's get the rest of those boxes so you can go home."

Halfway down the stairs, following Mother, Abby realized she'd done it again. Changing the subject seemed to be Mother's mode today. Because she didn't want to think about the selling of the house that had been in the family for over a hundred years, Abby didn't press. A half hour later, they finished the cleanup. As Abby got herself a glass of water, Mother came into the kitchen.

"Put the kettle on, and let's have some tea."

Abby silently groaned. All she wanted to do was go home and put her feet up. Spending all day with Mother had been too much for her. Still, she put the teakettle on the front grate of the gas stove, one of the few improvements in the house that had seen four generations of Jennings and Ten Eycks raised there. Some, like her grandmother, had even been born in the big Victorian.

While waiting for the kettle to boil, Abby brought teacups to the table. Generations of women in her family insisted that tea be drunk out of fine china cups. No mugs for the Jennings and Ten Eyck women. Abby didn't care. She'd drink tea or coffee out of a mug. Since Mother drank her tea the English way, Abby brought milk to the table, too.

"Be sure to rinse the teapot out with boiling water before you put in the tea."

Abby sighed. "Mother, I know how to prepare tea." After rinsing out the pot, putting in the teabags, then filling the pot with more boiling water, she brought the teapot to the table.

"Get the cozy out of the china cabinet drawer. Don't let the heat escape."

"Mother, what is wrong with you? I've been making tea since Grandma Jennings taught me when I was ten." After grabbing the padded tea cozy out of the dining room, she fitted it over the pot and finally sat down. "Okay. What's going on?"

Mother fiddled with the spoon next to her saucer. Abby hadn't brought one for herself. She liked her tea without any enhancements—no milk, no lemon, no sugar. Just plain tea.

"I had a boyfriend before your father."

That came out of nowhere. Since Abby didn't know where this new topic was headed, she waited. Mother looked at her expectantly.

"I assumed you did. You didn't marry Father until you were twenty-two."

"Oh. I see what you mean." Mother lifted the cozy then the lid and checked the tea. She poured each of them a cup. Apparently, stalling for time.

O-kay. What was the big deal?

"Grandmother Jennings said you were popular in high school. I figured that meant you had several boyfriends." She took a sip of the tea. A little strong for her taste. Mother would like it, diluted with milk.

"Those were for practice." Mother laughed, a nervous laugh. "That's what my mother called it. But I had another boyfriend. Someone I wanted to marry. We, uh, we were so sure we would marry that we, uh, anticipated our wedding vows."

Oh, my goodness. My prim and proper mother went all the way with a guy she didn't marry. Abby kept her expression neutral. "Why are you telling me this?"

"The cards and letters in that box are from him."

"I sort of figured that out when you went ballistic." Abby took a deep breath. "I assume the journals are from that time, too."

"They are. I want you to promise me something, Abigail." Mother reached across the table and clasped Abby's hand. "I want you to burn everything in that box."

"O-kay."

"Without reading."

CHAPTER TWO

For days after Mother's revelation, Abby was too busy with customers to think about it. At night, lying in bed, she pondered her mother's request. Could she do that? Burn the contents of the box without reading? Mother's insistence went beyond a request. She demanded a vow from Abby. Stalling, Abby had said she'd think about it.

With the holiday season in full swing, each day at the shop became busier than the one before. Often, she had to force a smile as she thanked each customer before rushing to help the next. By the end of the day, her back and feet hurt more than usual.

Murphy's Law kicked in two weeks after Thanksgiving. A shipment of holiday items went astray. Her regular delivery driver had broken his leg. The substitute driver, who was retired and should have stayed that way, said he'd delivered it and insisted she'd signed for it. After explaining for the tenth time that she hadn't received the delivery, she engaged in a shouting match with the surly old man. In the middle of the altercation, a good-looking guy sauntered in and cast her an inquiring glance. Considering the driver was shouting in her face, Mr. Good-Looking seemed concerned for her. That was a pleasant surprise. She shrugged, and he started browsing as far away from the back of the store as possible.

Abby shut her mouth, but the driver continued his harangue about shopkeepers who couldn't keep track of their deliveries. Finally, she asked—as politely as possible—to see her signature. He refused, saying his word should be good enough.

"Then my word should be good enough for *you*," Abby retorted. "I didn't receive the package."

He glared at her and snarled, "You must have. You just can't keep track of your own packages."

Gritting her teeth, she knew she wouldn't get anywhere with him. The holidays stressed out many people, and companies often hired warm bodies to keep up with demand. She thanked him for the packages he'd brought in. He grumbled as he left.

"Wait. I didn't sign—"

The slamming back door cut her off.

"Would you like me to go after him?" the customer asked in a soft baritone. *When had he migrated to the counter?*

"No." She realized how abrupt that sounded and said, "Thank you. I will call the depot and let them know what happened. After all his blustering, he forgot to have me sign for these packages." She waved at the tower of boxes he'd left on the floor blocking her in. "How can I help you?"

"I wanted to ask you about some miniatures you have in the window. But you, uh, might have a problem."

Dang it. She couldn't get out from behind the register without moving the boxes.

"No problem. I'll be with you in a minute." She took the top two boxes, thankfully light, and set them on the counter.

When she reached for the next box, the stranger had already picked it up along with the next two.

"You don't have to do that."

He grinned. "Many hands make the labor light. My mother used to say that." Chuckling, he moved the last two boxes. "Now, you're free."

The bell rang as two customers entered. Abby called out, "Good afternoon, Miz Rider, Miss Nickleson. Be right with you." She turned to the man. "About those miniatures?"

"Go ahead and help the ladies. I'm not in a hurry." His warm smile was so engaging she returned it.

"Thank—"

"Abigail, did my special order come in?" Harriet Nickleson had been Abby's eleventh grade history teacher. Miss Nickleson was a born teacher, who commanded attention in and out of the classroom. Abby often felt like a sixteen-year-old instead of a woman on the downhill side of thirty.

"One minute." She held up her index finger then turned to the computer next to the cash register. "Let me check."

Of all the special orders to go missing, it had to be Miss Nickleson's. Abby checked the computer again in case she'd made a mistake. She hadn't.

"I'm sorry. The order should have come in on Monday." The day her package went missing.

"It's Thursday." Miss Nickleson tapped her short no-nonsense nails on the counter.

"Yes, ma'am. I know. I promise I'll call you when your order comes in. Is there anything else I can help you with?"

"No. I came in specifically for my order. If it doesn't come in tomorrow, you might as well cancel it. It will never get to my nephew in Topeka in time for Christmas."

Abby took a breath and willed herself not to reply in kind. "Miss Nickleson, when you order arrives, I will wrap it and send it next day air so he gets his gift in time." Never mind it was more than two weeks until Christmas. Even with the increase in deliveries, he would get it before Santa came down the chimney.

"Hmph," the retired teacher grumbled. "I will want to see it first—to be sure it's what I ordered."

"Now, Harriet, don't be rude. Abby dear is trying her best."

With a grateful smile, Abby turned her attention to Freda Rider. "What can I help you with, Miz Rider?"

Freda waved her hand. "I just came in with Harriet. But, you know . . . " She glanced off to her left. "I thought I saw . . ."

When she turned to leave, Harriet Nickleson stalled her then lowered her voice. "Is that the man who moved here from New York City? With his father?"

Gossipy woman. With a mental chiding, Abby shook her head. "I wouldn't know."

"Don't be snippy, Abigail Ten Eyck. I wasn't talking to you. Freda, what do you think?"

"I don't know." Freda Rider kept her voice low. "I heard he's a millionaire who made a killing on Wall Street. And his father—"

"Freda, you're gossiping," Harriet chided. Never mind she was the one to start it.

Despite the two women attempting to keep their conversation to themselves, Abby knew how voices carried, especially voices of older women whose hearing wasn't what it used to be.

"Did you say you saw something, Miz Rider?"

The bell rang and a young mother with a baby in a front carrier and a toddler in tow rushed in. Dottie Matthews. If it had been anyone else, Abby would have feared for her breakables. Dottie had a death grip on the little boy, while the baby slept against her breast.

"Abby, I need a gift for—" She stopped. "Mrs. Rider, Miss Nickleson. How are you?"

The toddler yanked on his mother's slacks. "Mommy, I gotta go pee."

"Abs?" Dottie pleaded.

Abby jerked her head to the back room. How could she say no to a desperate little boy? Or his equally desperate mother.

The two older women took advantage of the distraction and left the shop. But, not before Miss Nickleson made a point about Abby calling her. Finally, she could deal with her lone customer. She approached the man.

"You were asking about miniatures? Oh, that's a beautiful one." She nodded at the tiny old-fashioned treadle sewing machine in his hand.

His smile made a dimple appear in his left cheek. "I was admiring the workmanship. Do you have any more from that company?"

"I don't think so. They're so expensive I don't order very many at a time. I have a catalog. Keep browsing while I look." She headed back to the counter.

Dottie and her little boy came up to her. "Thanks, Abs. I knew Billy wouldn't make it home. Dry," she whispered the last word. Continuing to whisper, she said, "I can't believe you mentioned how expensive something is. Don't you know who he is? He's loaded."

"What's loaded mean, Mommy?" His voice could be heard out on the sidewalk.

Dottie blushed and beat it out of the store.

"I see my reputation has preceded me." Again, the soft baritone sent a little shiver through Abby.

"You heard?"

"Not just your friend, but the older women, too." He chuckled. "That one was rather nasty to you."

Abby smiled before checking the store. It would be her luck to have another customer hear her gossip. "My high school history teacher . . . who still thinks I'm a student. Let's check that catalog."

After looking through the catalogs under the counter, she finally found the correct one. "I can special order anything you'd like."

As he leaned on the counter to peruse the catalog, the overhead light picked up a few silver hairs amid the dark strands. When he glanced up, heat filled her face at being caught staring at him. The bell announced a customer, and she gladly turned away. What was she doing staring at that man?

"I'll be right back," she assured him. "Hello, ladies. How can I help you?"

After ringing up more purchases, she realized the man had left. *Dang*. A missed sale. More customers entered, browsed, questioned, and some even bought. Before she knew it, her stomach declared that she'd missed lunch. While she ate an energy bar, she straightened the counter. Tucked under one of the boxes on the counter, she found the catalog, anchored by the miniature sewing machine. A piece of paper stuck out of the catalog. The list of items, including catalog numbers, totaled more than her receipts from the previous day. Holy cow, the man *was* rich.

Even better, he'd signed the list. Now she had a name to go with the face.

Sam Watson strolled down Main Street. He nodded and smiled at those bustling around him.

Most returned his smile. Others even greeted him with "Merry Christmas" or "Good afternoon." How different from New York City where people hurried down sidewalks and avoided eye contact. The last time he'd been out with his dad, people greeted him by name. But then, George had come out to Far Haven earlier than Sam and joined the Senior Center. Within days, he'd become part of the community.

Sam hadn't inherited that ability to make friends anywhere.

When Dad first talked about moving to the west side of Michigan, Sam's skepticism had kicked in. Why leave the house and neighborhood in Ann Arbor where he'd lived for years? "Memories," Dad had replied. "Time to let go of the past and move on."

Sam had wondered why it had taken him so long after Mom died. Four years since her funeral. Six, since her mind had become so clouded she didn't recognize the men she loved. Alzheimer's was a cruel bitch.

"Hi, there," a voice called out. "Aren't you George's son?"

A wiry man interrupted Sam's thoughts. *Good.* He didn't need to dwell on the past.

"Is everything all right, son?" the man asked.

Sam stopped and shook the man's hand. "Sam Watson. Yes, George is my dad."

"Dean Rider. Your dad plays in our bunco group. Glad to finally meet the boy he brags about. You were some big-time stock trader, I hear."

Sam chuckled, feeling the usual heat on the back of his neck whenever George talked about his success. That success landed him in the hospital. Twice.

"*Former* trader. Nice to meet you, Mr. Rider."
He tried to extricate himself.

"Dean. Call me Dean. Good to meet you, too."
The man leaned in close. "Got any hot tips?"

"Buy low, sell high."

For a moment, Dean stared. Then he laughed.
"Good one. You're a corker, all right. Just like your
dad." He shivered. "Damn cold."

He was right about that. Even through his
heavy winter coat, Sam felt the chill that came off
Lake Michigan.

"Been looking for my wife. She was supposed
to meet me an hour ago. Have you seen her? About
this high—" He held his hand up next to his ear. "—
and this round." He held his arms out in a wide
circle. "Don't tell her I did that. She met up with
Harriet Nickleson. Those two can't tell time."

Sam remembered the two ladies in the gift
shop. "I saw them at Gifts & More." He glanced at
his watch then gave Dean a look of chagrin. "That
was about two hours ago. Sorry."

"Never mind. I'm going to wait in the café.
They can find me for a change." Dean headed down
the street. After a few steps, he turned around. "You
have a good day, now."

After three weeks, Sam hadn't grown
accustomed to the friendliness of the small town.
Even the woman at the gift shop, Abby, was warm
and friendly. He'd witnessed her pleasantness
firsthand. Of course, that was her business, and it
behooved her to be friendly to customers. It went
beyond that, though. Even when her former teacher
scolded her, she kept her smile. And a charming
smile it was.

"I talked to Maureen Donovan yesterday."

Mother's announcement startled Abby so much, she nearly dropped her cup of tea. Maureen owned Donovan Realty and was the best real estate agent in Far Haven.

"About Spring Fest?" Abby put as much innocence into her question as she could.

Ever since Thanksgiving, Mother had grumbled about the big, old Victorian. Abby had ignored the complaints, convincing herself she misunderstood what Mother was hinting at. She still hoped the two women had chatted about the May festival. They both served on the steering committee.

Mother set her fine china cup back in its saucer. "Not about Spring Fest." She paused. "After New Year's, I'm putting the house up for sale. Maureen says lakefront property goes quickly."

Abby's heart went cold. Not her home. Mother couldn't do that.

"It's too much upkeep," she went on. "Ever since your father passed, this house is so empty. Too empty. Too much work."

Carefully, Abby placed her cup in the saucer. They sat at the small kitchen table in the nook overlooking Lake Michigan and Mother's garden— her pride and joy—now snow-covered and stark, without the cheery colors of the lovely flowers that would grace the backyard from early spring to late fall.

"Mother, you have a cleaning service. If you need them more often . . ."

"It's not just the cleaning, dear, or the snow removal and lawncare." She'd beaten Abby to the punch by being the first to mention those services.

"What's really going on? You can't just drop a bombshell like that on me and expect me to be happy. This is the house I grew up in—my home."

Why did she pick two days before Christmas to announce this?

Mother reached across the corner of the table to cover Abby's hand. "Your home is above your shop, with Bethany. And someday—" She took a deep breath. "—with your husband."

Abby made a rude noise. "Not going to be another husband. Not after Ferret Face. I mean it, Mother. You can't sell our home."

"Hate to break it to you, kiddo. I can."

CHAPTER THREE

The ringing of her phone that night had Abby scrambling across the covers to the nightstand where she'd plugged in her cell phone. Two-oh-one blazed from the bedside clock in three-inch high red numerals. She yanked her phone off the charger. In her hurry, she hoped she hadn't bent the prongs. Dang, the things you had to worry about with new technology.

"Hello." Her voice sounded groggy, so she cleared her throat. "Hello?"

"Abby? This is Rose at the police station."

Oh dear God. Bethany. She'd gone out on a date with a new boy. Tom something or other. But Abby was certain she'd heard her daughter come in earlier.

"What happened?" As she clutched the cell phone, she had no idea how she could speak with her heart yammering in her ears.

"I'm calling about your mother. She's all right," the dispatcher said quickly, as if to reassure her.

How can anyone be reassured when the police call you at two a.m.? A ringing phone at that hour never brought good news.

"My mother?"

"Yes. She's been arrested."

Oh, dear God. What had Mother done?
"Arrested? For what?"

"Trespassing on private property. And theft."

The phone fell from Abby's boneless fingers. It hit the nightstand then landed on the hardwood floor and skidded under the bed. Ever since Mother dropped the bomb earlier that day about selling the house, Abby had worried about her. But trespassing and . . . theft? Did she need money that badly? Is that why she wanted to sell the house? What—

"Hello? Abby, are you there?" Rose's faint voice interrupted Abby's speculation.

Leaning over the edge of the bed, she patted the floor until she scooped up the phone. "Yes, I'm here. Thanks, Rose. I'll be right down."

"Uh, Abby? Florence doesn't want you to come. In fact, she didn't want me to call you."

Her sleep-deprived mind wasn't operating at full efficiency. "What? Not come? I don't understand."

"I knew you'd want to know. This isn't an official call. She says she's saving her one phone call for someone important."

Someone important? That sure puts me in my place. "Then don't tell her I'm coming."

As Abby pulled on her old jeans, the ones she'd thrown over the treadmill last night, a sleepy-eyed, yawning Bethany knocked lightly on the open bedroom door. Her long brown hair stuck out around her face like a dandelion.

"What's going on, Mom? It's two in the morning. Why are you getting dressed?"

Abby didn't bother changing out of her long-sleeve sleep shirt, nor did she waste time tucking it into her jeans. "Grandma's in jail."

"What?" That yanked the sleep out of her daughter's eyes. "What happened?"

"I'll tell all when I come back." She shoved her feet into her flannel-lined clogs.

"I'm coming with you." Bethany ran back to her room yelling, "Don't leave without me."

Aggravated at having to wait while her daughter dressed, Abby grabbed her winter jacket out of the front closet. She smushed her hair into her orange and blue Hope College watch cap. She'd taken the keys off the hook next to the door to the back stairs when Bethany skidded across the hall floor in her sock-clad feet. Smart girl, unlike Abby who hadn't taken time to put socks on. She was too anxious to hear what her mother had been up to that ended with her arrest for trespassing and, worse, theft. Clenching her teeth, Abby knew her mother's version of what she'd done would vary greatly from the deputy's. She just hoped the arresting officer wasn't Deputy Dawg. That man was a menace to anyone he went to high school with, even those a few years older—like Abby and the boys in her class.

With Bethany tromping in heavy boots down the stairs behind her, several scenarios raced through Abby's mind—each worse than the one before. Mother didn't have a lick of common sense when it came to other people's property, especially if she knew the person. Considering she'd lived in Far Haven all her life, she knew almost everyone. She'd have a perfectly good (according to her) explanation for trespassing.

Theft was another matter. That's what bothered Abby the most. What had she stolen? How valuable? More importantly, why? Mother had a good income from Father's investments. She might sound like a scatterbrain sometimes, but Mother managed her money well. At least, Abby thought she did.

Downstairs, Abby wrestled with the wind as she tried to open the back door. Bethany helped and together they got it open then closed and latched tight. The same wind cut through her winter coat as she slogged through a snowdrift. *Dang, I should have worn socks.* And boots. Snow and wind froze her feet before she could get into her van parked behind the store. Though it was convenient to live above her shop, on nights like this, she would love to have an attached garage. Snow blowing in from the south had drifted against her vehicle. By the time she got inside, her wet pant legs clung to her calves. She gritted her teeth against the icy-cold that filled her clogs.

Bethany jumped into the passenger's side, stomping her boots on the frame to knock off the snow. "You can tell me why Gram is in jail on the way."

"I suppose I could . . . if I knew." Her hands shook from the cold as she stabbed the key into the ignition. After a false start, the engine finally turned over. The blowing cold air made her wish she had a newer vehicle—one with remote start. She could have started the van upstairs while waiting for Bethany, and heat would be pouring out of the vents instead of frigid air.

She backed out onto the street, nearly getting hung up on the large pile of snow. *Dang*, the plows had been out already and buried the driveway. Old Faithful bumped over the drift and fishtailed out onto Third Street. The springs and shocks had seen better days and needed to be replaced. If she could afford it, she'd replace Old Faithful. Something she never said out loud for fear of jinxing the fifteen-year-old Chevy van. The faded tan paint job was nothing glamorous, but the vehicle had been reliable transportation from the get-go. Abby wouldn't disparage the van that had served her and her business well for the past ten years.

"Mo-om?" From Bethany's exasperated tone, she'd been trying to get Abby's attention.

"Yes. Sorry. What did you say?"

"Aren't you worried about Gram?"

"Of course, I am," she snapped then blew out a breath. "I'm sorry, sweetie. Your grandmother is going to drive me into an early grave."

She hadn't told her daughter about Mother's plan to sell her house. Just because that ruined Abby's Christmas didn't mean she had to ruin Bethany's.

Taking a page out of her mother's book, Abby asked, "How was your date last night?" *How's that for changing the subject?* She'd learned from the best.

Bethany wobbled her hand. "So-so. He didn't know how to carry on a conversation."

"Some guys are shy. Is he that way at school?"

"Well, he is kind of quiet. He doesn't shoot his mouth off like Logan did."

"Is that why you broke up with Logan?"

"Not really. We just decided to see other people." She took a breath then exclaimed, "You pulled a *Grandma.*"

"A what?"

"You don't want to explain why Grandma's in jail, so you changed the subject. Just like she does."

Abby reached over and squeezed Bethany's knee. "You are too observant, young lady. Honestly, I don't know. We have to wait until we get to the jail."

Over snow-covered and slippery streets on the way to the Far Haven police station, she told Bethany as much as she knew. Ever since Father died, Mother had changed. And not in a good way. First, she turned in the lovely silver Lincoln he'd bought her right before he died for a red Mustang, and a convertible, at that. Then she'd dyed her hair blonde. *Blonde*, for God's sake. Father hated dyed hair. He said natural was better. Mother claimed that *was* her natural color, pre-gray. Abby couldn't believe the change. With a stylish new cut, Mother looked younger and more vibrant.

Abby hated change.

Worse, she kept thinking about Mother selling the house—the home of Ten Eycks and Jennings for over a hundred years. Too much upkeep sounded like an excuse. What else was going on? Abby had lain awake past midnight the night before and again that night trying to figure it out. Her heart ached at the thought of someone else living in the house in which she'd grown up. If only . . .

No. She'd learned long ago "if onlys" were a waste of time. No sense dwelling on what one couldn't change.

She pulled up in front of the red brick Public Safety building—police and fire departments, all in one. Far Haven was too small for more. As she and Bethany struggled to leave the van, the wind off Lake Michigan buffeted them. Combined with the snow-covered parking lot, Abby had a hard time remaining upright. Another reminder that she should've worn her boots. The wind had picked up since leaving home, almost gale force.

Clutching each other, she and Bethany staggered into the station. The wind made the door hard to open and even harder to close behind them. They stomped their feet on the mat to rid the snow and ice. Rose sat in her usual place of honor surrounded by closed circuit monitors that showed the front of the building, doors, hallways, and the jail cells.

She looked up from her computer. Though that monitor was angled away, it looked like Rose had been playing solitaire. What else could she do while waiting for emergency calls? Far Haven wasn't exactly a hotbed of crime. Not in the winter, anyway. Summer was a different story.

Abby's attention was drawn back to the other monitors. What—

"Abby. Bethie." Rose insisted on thinking her daughter was still the toddler she used to babysit. "Sorry to call you out on such a nasty night."

As much as she liked Rose, Abby didn't have time for polite chit-chat. She scanned the room, expecting to find her mother sitting at one of the deputy's desks. "Where's my mother?"

A blush flooded Rose's face. "Deputy Dawson locked her up."

"In jail? My mother's in jail?" Abby craned her neck to look closer then pointed at a monitor. "Is that Mother? Who's with her?"

Bethany patted her shoulder. "Mom, don't go ballistic on Auntie Rose. It's not her fault."

"No, it's that dang Deputy Dawg. Wait until I get my hands on that idiot. Where is he?"

"Now, now, dear. Listen to Bethie." Rose took a set of keys out of her drawer. "Ron is out tending to a couple of fender-benders. You wouldn't believe the calls tonight. Come, I'll take you back to see Florence."

In all the time Abby had lived in Far Haven—thirty-six years minus the two away when she was married to Ferret Face—she'd never seen the inside of the jail. In fact, she'd never seen the inside of any jail.

Rose led them down a beige hall. At the end, she unlocked a metal-barred door set into the wall on the left. They walked down a shorter hall, and there it was. The jail, two cells complete with steel bars, a narrow cot and a stainless-steel commode in each. Mother sat on the edge of the cot at the back of the cell.

As Abby had seen in the monitor, she wasn't alone.

"Who are you?" Abby demanded of the old man sitting next to Mother. And holding her mother's hand!

Florence bounded off the cot with the agility of a much younger woman. All those classes at the Senior Center must be paying off. "Abigail Louise, what are you doing here?"

Abby fisted her hands on her hips. "What are *you* doing in jail? And who is that man?"

That man rose more slowly than Mother had. He looked to be about her age, or slightly older, and a little taller with a head of thick, gray hair and a weathered face that had seen a lot of sun. When he reached Mother's side, he placed his arm around her waist. *Around her waist! How dare he?*

"Rose." Florence gripped the steel bars, indignation in her voice as well as in her piercing stare. "I specifically told you not to call Abigail. I will never speak to you again."

"You'll have to talk to me at bridge," the dispatcher quipped before she beat it back down the hall.

"Don't count on it, you traitor. And, you, Abigail. Go home. I don't want you here. How could you drag poor Bethany out of bed at this hour of the morning? And it's such a nasty night with the storm coming in across the lake."

With that, her mother returned to the cot. The old man shrugged and gave Abby an apologetic half smile before joining Florence.

"At least have the courtesy to tell me what is going on, Mother."

When Bethany elbowed her, Abby shot her daughter the same glare her mother had given her.

"I want to know what you were doing to get arrested."

"Yeah," a deep baritone behind her said. "I'd like to know what she did that got *my father* arrested."

Abby spun around. Apparently, Rose had escorted another visitor—a tall, dark-haired man. It took her a moment before she recognized the man from the store, the one who ordered those miniatures. Sam Watson.

"More likely your father instigated the whole thing," she shot back.

"I'll let you folks straighten things out. I have to get back to the phones," Rose said before making a hasty retreat.

"Mom, calm down. Let's listen to Gram and . . . his father." Bethany jerked her head toward Sam.

They hadn't formally met, despite the fact that he'd come to her store twice. He'd returned to pay for the special order. A nice boost to Abby's bottom line. But with all the customers coming and going, they'd had little time to talk. From the rumors, she'd learned he was a "retired" stock trader now a furniture maker. Considering the sawdust and wood shavings clinging to his flannel shirt and the front of his jeans, the last part must be true.

"Sam, my boy." The old man walked slowly forward. From his grimace, arthritis must be taking its toll on his bones. "You didn't need to come."

"Sure I did, Dad. Now would someone tell me what's going on? Why are you in jail?"

"We-ell, Flo here fell into a dumpster behind—"

"A dumpster?" Abby exclaimed. "Mo-ther. What were you doing in a dumpster?"

Mother rushed to the bars. "Don't you talk to me like that, young lady."

Sam glared at Abby. "We'll get the story quicker if you let my father talk."

Abby planted her hands on her hips. "How will we know it's the truth? He could make up a story so my mother will look stupid."

"Mo-om." Bethany tried to hush her.

"Abigail Louise Ten Eyck, don't you talk about George like that."

"Oh, for God's sake. Everybody be still." Sam raked his hand through his dark hair. "Dad, tell us what happened. Then, Flo, you tell your side."

Flo? Nobody called Mother *Flo.* Father had not approved of nicknames. *Hang on.* How did he know Mother well enough to call her anything?

"I wish all of you would go home," Mother said. "George and I are perfectly all right."

"Tomorrow is Christmas Eve."

"It's tomorrow already, Mom." Bethany gave her a little smile.

"You're right." Abby felt so discombobulated. "Well, Mother, you are not spending Christmas Eve in jail."

Florence jutted out her chin. "I'll do what I damn well please, Abigail."

Sam Watson rubbed his rough jaw. He'd worked so late finishing his latest project he'd fallen across the bed, fully dressed. Given the urgency of the late-night phone call, he hadn't bothered to change clothes. The bristling woman standing next to him looked to be in the same shape—roused from sleep by a late night phone call.

Dad had told him Flo and her daughter had an adversarial relationship. He just hadn't mentioned how bad it was. Or maybe he hadn't known. Dad hadn't met the daughter until now.

At this moment, Abby could be her mother's clone. Same mutinous expression, same defensiveness. But, where Flo always had a ready smile, the daughter looked aggravated and worried. As she should be. He was worried, too.

With a furled brow, creases along her mouth, and thinned lips, she looked different from when he'd been in Gifts & More. For her customers, she had a ready smile. A cute smile. Ever since he saw her in the shop, he'd meant to talk to her more—more than a thank you after she rang up his special order. But each time he'd gone into her shop, she'd been too busy to talk.

Under her open navy jacket, she wore what looked like a pink sleepshirt—with little dancing dogs—over well-worn jeans and bare feet stuffed into green plaid flannel-lined clogs. In her hand, she carried an orange watch cap. He wondered if she knew how mussed her hair was, from sleep and static electricity. The few times he'd seen her, that sable brown hair had been scraped back from her face and twisted into a fancy bun. Or bundled up with one of those claw-like things. He liked this free style better.

Ever since Dad started dating Flo, Sam hadn't understood Flo's reluctance to introduce them to her daughter. He'd wanted to officially meet Abby. Just not like this.

Dad cleared his throat. "Like I started to say, Flo fell into a dumpster behind the bakery. She was trying to get one more loaf of bread."

"Bread? You were dumpster diving for bread?" Abby's voice echoed off the walls of the enclosed area. "Is that why you want to sell the house? You need the money? If you're so desperate for food, Mother, you should have told me."

"Time out." The teen made the universal "t" sign. "What's this about selling your house? Grandma, you can't." Tears shimmered in her eyes.

"Oh, Bethie." Flo reached between the bars to clasp her granddaughter's hand. "It's for the best. But not until after the holidays. And I guess not until we're out of jail."

"Off topic," Sam reminded them. "I want to know what you two did to get arrested."

Not to be deterred, Bethany clung to her grandmother's hand. "But getting food for yourself isn't the reason for taking the bread out of a dumpster, is it, Gram?"

Ah, the sensible one in the trio of Ten Eyck women . . . and the least volatile. The girl, with her mother's sky-blue eyes, had darker brown hair and looked about seventeen. She wore a Far Haven High School Marching Band jacket. He thought Dad told him she was a senior and played clarinet. She also had a good influence on both her grandmother and her mother with her soft, reasonable voice. She hadn't learned that from either of the older women.

"No, Bethany dear. The bread isn't for me." Flo sighed. "It's for the birds. That stingy Duncan won't give me the stale bread, so I have to take it out of his trash bin."

"Now, Flo," Dad said. "You know he isn't being stingy. He can't give anybody the old bread. If they ate it and got sick, they might sue him."

Flo harrumphed. "So you've said several times."

"I don't understand how you ended up in the dumpster, too, Dad."

His mouth twisted and red crept up his neck. "I was trying to help her out and . . . Well, Flo doesn't know her own strength."

She grinned up at Sam. "I've been taking classes at the Senior Center and using the machines in the equipment room. I can lift fifty pounds." She raised her arm and made a muscle.

Sam bit his lip to keep from smiling. Flo was a hoot. No wonder his dad enjoyed her company. "I understand the trespassing part of your arrest. Where does the theft come in?"

"Duncan Randolph instructed me to arrest anyone taking anything from his property."

Abby, her daughter, and Sam all turned to look at the newcomer. Deputy Ron Dawson escorted a drunk into the adjoining cell. The deputy glared at them. Sam had heard he was a whiz with the radar gun. So far, he'd avoided being stopped.

"Ron Dawson, you let my mother out of jail right now." Again, Abby fisted her hands on her hips.

"No can do." Dawson sneered. "Randolph is adamant."

"Once something is thrown in the trash, isn't it fair game?" Sam asked.

"Don't know, don't care." Dawson drew himself up straighter than a Marine at attention.

"Where is Chief Hoesen?" Abby demanded. "He will sort things out and release my mother."

"The chief is on vacation. He won't be back until after Christmas." Dawson puffed out his chest. "I'm in charge."

"Heaven help Far Haven," she muttered.

"What was that?" Dawson demanded.

"Clean out your ears, Dawg," Abby shot back.

They bickered like little kids, Sam thought in disgust. He needed to get things back on track. "How do we post bail?"

"The judge will decide bail at the hearing," Dawson, still filled with self-importance, announced with a smug look.

Abby took a deep breath then asked, "And when will the hearing take place?"

At least she'd toned down her anger. That woman was going to have a stroke or ulcers if she didn't learn to manage her emotions better. Sam knew all about the dangers of stress.

"December twenty-sixth."

"I can't believe that man." Abby turned the key in the ignition. The van didn't start. Just ground away, slower and slower each time.

"Which one?" Bethany fastened her seatbelt. "Deputy Dawg, Grandma's date, or the cute guy?"

"Do not call Deputy Dawson—wait. What cute guy?" As if she didn't know. Sam Watson was one good looking man.

"C'mon, Mom. Don't tell me you didn't notice Sam. Mister Tall, Dark, and Ruggedly Handsome? Yum-my."

"Bethany Ann, he is way too old for you." Hoping that would deter Bethany from a dangerous train of thought, she tried to start the car again.

"Me? You have got to be kidding. I was thinking for you."

As if she had any real interest in a man, no matter how handsome. Ferret Face had cured her of that. Abby blew out an exasperated noise. "Dang car. I hope Triple A isn't too busy."

Leaning forward for access, she dug her phone out of her back pocket. A rap on her window made her jump. Her cell flew in the air and bounced on the dash. She bobbled it twice until it landed in Bethany's lap.

Sam Watson stood outside, his hands in his jacket pockets, his breath frosting in the air. He made a roll-down-the-window gesture.

With no power, she couldn't. She had to open the door. "What?"

"Mo-om," Bethany whispered. "You sound like a bi-witch." That was their preferred epithet to replace the vulgar one.

"Car trouble?" Sam asked.

"No trouble." She gave him a tight smile. "I love sitting in a cold car in thirty below windchill at four in the morning."

Bethany leaned across the gearshift, dropping Abby's cell in her lap. "Yes, our car won't start. Mom was going to call road service."

She wanted to poke her daughter in the ribs for announcing their vulnerability. Still, she had to be practical. Sitting in a dead car waiting for road service wasn't healthy for Bethany. Or herself. She glanced up at him. In the few moments standing next to her van, snow had covered Sam's hair and long lashes. *Wait. Since when do I notice a man's eyelashes?*

He shoved his hands into his tan Carhartt jacket pockets. "The dispatcher said the storm is causing havoc on the roads. I imagine it will take a long time for anyone to get here. I can give you a ride home."

Before Abby could respond, Bethany eagerly accepted his offer. She jumped out of the car, leaving Abby sitting behind the steering wheel. *What a rotten night.* She hadn't had one like this since she caught Ferret Face and his girlfriend doing the naughty in her bed.

Sam continued to stand outside her door. "Abby, I'm not the bad guy in this scenario. Are you coming?"

No, he wasn't the bad guy. He seemed genuinely concerned about her and Bethany. Just as he'd been about his father. Rather than seem ungrateful, she climbed out of her car, promptly slipped on a snowy patch, and nearly landed on her butt. Sam caught her in time. One of her clogs slipped off and flew several feet away then slid a few more feet on the icy parking lot.

Perfect. Just perfect.

Sam said, "Hold onto your van, while I get your shoe."

When he returned, he held onto her clog. "Allow me to play Prince Charming, Cinderella."

Oh, God. What a grin. Dang, he knew how to charm a girl. He must have women lining up for his bed.

Geez, could I have been any snarkier when he offered help? That made her even more embarrassed.

"Mademoiselle, s'il vous plait?" He held out the clog like a shoe salesman.

As if to make up for her earlier rudeness, she played along. "Oui, monsieur." Clinging to the door handle, she lifted her foot. Giving her another grin, he slid the shoe on.

With his arm around her waist, he helped her across the parking lot. So discombobulated by him holding her and the silly game with her clog, she couldn't speak. Thanks to his support, she managed to shuffle the short distance and up into his SUV. His warm SUV. When he got in beside her— Bethany had taken the backseat—the interior seemed a lot smaller.

"You live above your shop on Main, don't you?" he asked as he put his vehicle into gear.

"You seem to know a lot about us." As soon as she said it, she realized she'd gone back to *bi-witch* mode. "I'm sorry. You don't deserve my bad mood. Our entrance is on the Third Street side."

He easily maneuvered the big vehicle around the slippery streets. "Getting a call at two in the morning never brings good news, does it? Especially from the police."

She turned to him. "That's exactly what I thought when I got the call."

"Kindred spirits?" The deep rumble of his laugh was contagious. "Your mother talks about you two a lot. She says Bethany is an honor student, and you work too hard."

She'd heard that before. Too many times to count. "My mother never mentioned you or your father. How long has she been seeing him?"

"Mo-om."

She must have reverted to the *bi-witch*. "Sorry. This has been a crazy night."

"I know. What are we going to do about our parents?"

"They can't stay in jail over Christmas," Bethany exclaimed. "We could break them out. I saw where Auntie Rose keeps the keys. You guys could distract her, and I could unlock the cell and help them escape out the back door."

Abby sputtered while Sam chuckled. He spoke first. "That might work. But then we'd all spend Christmas in jail."

Bethany propped her arms on the back of the front seat. "Do you have a better suggestion?"

"We are not going to break them out of jail," Abby pronounced. "If it wasn't Christmas Eve, I'd say Mother should learn her lesson about dumpster diving."

"You don't mean that, Mom. We'd have to eat that huge turkey all by ourselves."

Next to her, the big man chuckled. She had to admit his laughter made her smile. Something she hadn't done in a long while. And his game with her flying clog. Cinderella, indeed. For a moment, she grinned.

At ten in the morning, a mechanic from Schuyler Automotive brought her van around. Apparently, Sam had called and even paid for the service. Although she thought that was pretty high-handed of him, Abby was grateful for his thoughtfulness. But, she would pay him back. After the financial disaster of her marriage, Abby always paid her own way.

She and Bethany headed back to the police station. The sun had returned, and the winds off Lake Michigan had died down. That's the way it was with a storm. A blustery night followed by a beautiful day. This morning was no exception. Snow-coated evergreens looked almost artificial and the sun glinted off ice-covered branches.

Instead of Rose, Jenny Sampson sat at the dispatch desk. Far Haven was so small, the deputies—Jenny and Ron Dawson—took turns relieving Rose and each other. With the chief gone, they must be working double time.

"Hi, Abby. If you've come to see your mother, you're just in time. Ron's taking her and George Watson over to the courthouse."

At that moment, Deputy Dawg ushered a handcuffed George and Florence to the side door of the station, the one closest to the courthouse.

"Really, Ron?" Jenny said. "Handcuffs? Afraid those two desperados might get away from you?"

The deputy, who carried a large, black garbage bag, ignored her.

Abby said, "I didn't think the hearing was until Tuesday."

Jenny winked. "Somebody—who shall remain anonymous—called Judge DeVran before she went off duty. Ron had to come back to work to take them to the courthouse. After working all night, he is not a happy camper."

Abby wasn't real happy, either. Not with that little twerp, Dawg. He'd been a pain in the butt all the way through school. Thank goodness, he wasn't in her class. Being a few years older, she'd escaped the fate of her friends Alex O'Hara and Dottie Matthews, his usual victims.

She and Bethany raced around the block to the courthouse. When they arrived in the oak-paneled room, Sam dashed in behind her.

While she leaned against a bench, he bent over to catch his breath. "The hearing hasn't started yet, has it?"

As out of breath as him, she shook her head then pointed to the group at the front of the courtroom—George, Florence, and Deputy Dawg.

Abby followed Bethany into a bench. Sam slid in next to her. She tried to scoot over, but Bethany wouldn't budge. Abby was about to ask her to move when the bailiff announced, "All rise. The honorable Judge Daniel DeVran presiding."

Santa Claus walked out and sat on the bench.

CHAPTER FOUR

"Well, now. Is everyone here?" Santa asked. "Lawyers? Since this is such an important case?" His eyes twinkled beneath the white fur of his hat.

George stood. "Yes, sir. We're both here. We don't need lawyers."

"Yeah." Mother stood. "We don't need no stinkin' lawyers."

While George chuckled and Mother chortled over the movie quote, Abby wanted to crawl under the bench. The judge rolled his eyes.

"Deputy, get those ridiculous handcuffs off those two upstanding citizens. They are hardly likely to escape." As soon as the cuffs were removed, Judge Santa said, "Now, what is this all about?"

Dawson drew himself up. "Florence Ten Eyck and George Watson are accused of trespassing and theft. Here's the evidence." He held up the large bag then spilled the contents onto the table in front of the judge.

"Tell me, Deputy. Are those five loaves of bread? Where are the two fishes?" Again, his eyes twinkled, and he looked like he was trying not to laugh at his own joke.

"Yes, er, no. Sir." Dawg stumbled over his response. "I mean no fish. Just the bread. From the dumpster at Randolph's bakery."

Abby snorted softly. Bethany poked her in the side with her elbow.

"Florence and George, why were you taking bread from the dumpster? The Far Haven Mission feeds those in need."

"The bread isn't for us," George said. "We feed the ducks with it."

Mother stood. "Danny, I mean Your Honor. Sir. That stingy old Duncan Randolph wouldn't give me the bread when I asked him. We feed it to all the birds at Waterfront Park."

Judge DeVran's lips thinned. "Deputy, you called me away from my important duties at the hospital for this?" He shoved up his fur cuff to look at his watch.

"Yes, sir. I—"

"If Santa is late for the children's holiday party, it will be your fault, Deputy. Case dismissed." He banged the gavel then stood.

"But, sir—"

Santa narrowed his eyes. "Deputy Dawson, do you understand the words *case dismissed*?" He banged the gavel again.

"But—"

"Speak again, boy—" Santa shook the gavel at him. "—and you'll be the one spending Christmas in jail. Dismissed. Get out of here. All of you."

George and Florence stood and hugged each other, Santa left the room, and Deputy Dawg walked down the aisle with his tail between his legs, and the handcuffs on his belt jingling like the bells on Santa's sleigh.

Outside the courthouse, the bright sun made the snow-covered trees glisten like fairy-land. Florence hugged George again, then Sam and Bethany. She looked at Abby and sighed. "This was the most fun I've had in years. Don't ruin it with a lecture."

Abby thought of several things to say—none of them good. "It's okay, Mother." She gave her a quick hug. "Let's go home."

Mother said, "George, remember what I said when we were in the slammer. You and Sam come for Christmas dinner tomorrow. Abby's cooking at my house. Two o'clock and don't be late."

George grinned. "You've told me so much about Abby's prowess in the kitchen, I can't wait."

After Sam and George left, Abby turned on her mother. "Why did you invite them? Christmas is for family. Besides, we hardly know them."

She tipped her head to the side. "When did you become so mean spirited? Christmas is a time of sharing, especially with those in need. And, believe me, those two men need a good home-cooked meal. You're going to have to get used to George being around. Besides, I don't want those two bachelors eating Christmas dinner at Denny's or some such place."

As they got in the van, she pondered what her mother said. Was she being mean spirited for wanting to spend Christmas with only her immediate family? While Thanksgiving had always been a day for the gathering of relatives, usually at Mother's house, Father insisted Christmas was for the four of them. After Father died, Mother, Bethany, and she spent Christmas together.

Then the rest of what Mother said registered. "What do you mean we have to get used to George being around?"

"I love him."

Abby couldn't believe what she heard. Mother loved that man?

"That's really cool, Grandma. Are you going to marry him?"

Marry? Oh, Lord. Replace Father? No. Mother couldn't do that.

"Maybe, maybe not." Mother wobbled her hand. "We haven't figured that out yet."

"Hang on. How long have you known him? How could you know you're in love with a man you've just met?"

"Who says we just met?"

Stunned, Abby drove the rest of the way home in silence, barely taking in the conversation between her mother and her daughter. Mother was in love? Was that why she looked so happy? Was George the reason she'd changed so much? Abby should be happy for her. Instead, she felt numb and—dare she admit it—jealous.

The next afternoon Sam and his father walked up to the Ten Eyck home. As he did the first time, Sam paused on the red brick walkway and took in the beauty of the old Victorian house. Matching red brick with white trim and a wraparound porch, the house beckoned him, like an old friend welcoming him home. He shook off the fanciful thoughts. George beat him to the white door with a large, slightly off-center wreath.

Flo welcomed them both with a kiss. For Sam, a chaste buss on the cheek, while George's kiss led into an embrace. Not wanting to intrude, Sam shrugged off his coat. Flo then bustled about taking their coats and urging them to sit on the bench in the wide foyer and remove their boots. Bethany joined them, helping her grandmother hang up the outerwear in a closet nearly hidden behind a five-foot tall Norfolk pine, decorated with miniature ornaments. Sam marveled at how healthy the plant looked, evidence of Flo's green thumb.

While waiting for his dad to remove his boots, Sam gave an appreciative glance around the foyer. A crystal chandelier dispelled the gloom of winter by reflecting light off the gleaming marble floor, in the middle of which lay a red Persian-style rug. The gleaming white banister of the curving staircase caught his eye. A green garland was artfully draped along the rail, ending at the newel post with a red bow. Accenting the cherry wood steps, a runner in the same design as the rug, covered the treads, each anchored by a gold rod. Elegant, tasteful. Just like Flo.

Seeing his dad's difficulty in getting up from the bench, Sam offered a hand. As usual, George brushed it off, much the same as a toddler who wanted to do it himself. While he admired his dad's independence, he wished George would accept help—considering how he, Sam, had had to accept his dad's help earlier that year.

Abby walked out from the kitchen, smoothing a large apron that covered her glittery red sweater and black slacks. "Welcome. I hope you brought your appetites."

"We did, indeed." George walked up to her. "Merry Christmas." He hesitated, uncertain whether to kiss, hug, or shake hands.

Abby solved his problem by holding out her hand. "Merry Christmas, Mr. Watson." She nodded to Sam. "Merry Christmas to you, too. I'd better get back to the kitchen. Don't want dinner to burn."

Before Sam could shake her hand, she spun around and disappeared.

"Come into the living room." Flo gestured to her right. "Drinks and hors d'oeuvres await."

Sam had only been in this house once, shortly after he arrived in west Michigan. The living room was tastefully decorated for the holidays. The tree in front of the window had to be ten feet tall. With its twelve-foot ceiling, the room would have dwarfed a smaller tree. Intrigued by what looked like a mishmash of ornaments, he walked closer to examine them.

"I made that decoration when I was in kindergarten." Bethany had come up behind him and pointed to what looked like a butterfly made of wallpaper and a hairclip. "Mom made that one in preschool. And Gram made this one in grade school."

The last two ornaments, a Shrinky Dink star—Sam remembered making those—and a pinecone with glued glitter were amateurish and charming. Nadine would've disdained them, opting for matching ornaments, ribbons, and lights. Not this record of children's growth. His mother would have approved, though.

"Mom and I helped Gram decorate. She won't let Gram get up on a ladder."

"Good thing," George said. He, too, had come over to admire the tree. "Can't have my sweetie falling."

"Oh, you." Flo swiped her hand against his arm in a playful, yet intimate, gesture. "I love my tree. So many wonderful memories." This time she swiped at the moisture on her eyelashes. "Come, Sam, have a glass of Christmas cheer. George, you do the honors. Bethie, tell your mother to come out for a toast."

Sam would rather have examined the decorations. Instead, he opted to be a good guest. He snatched a cracker-laden canape before accepting a glass of ginger ale from his dad. Always discreet, George never talked about Sam no longer drinking alcohol.

Bethany returned from the kitchen, her mouth turned down. "Mom says to go ahead without her. She's afraid the sweet potatoes will burn if she doesn't watch them. I offered to help, but you know Mom." She glanced over at her grandmother who nodded with an expression that mirrored the teen. Disappointment and resignation.

Hiding out in the kitchen seemed to be a common occurrence for Abby. So did refusing help. He knew how that went. Old do-it-myself Sam had first-hand experience. The twinge in his belly reminded him of what happened when you tried to do everything yourself, when work consumed you. When your body attacked itself.

George held up a highball glass. "Here, Sam. If the mountain won't come . . . Take this out to Abby."

Despite the vent fan roaring at top speed, the heat from the oven and stovetop made the small room hotter than August. Abby raised her forearm to wipe the sweat off her brow and to push her damp hair off her face.

"Would you like a towel?" Sam stood in the doorway under the mistletoe Bethany had hung. He held two glasses, each containing an amber liquid.

"You startled me." Abby wouldn't admit she was happy to see him. Handsome in a rugged way, Sam exuded confidence and strength, necessary characteristics for a Mover-and-Shaker in the business world. She wondered again what he was doing in little Far Haven. Not exactly a hotbed of finance.

Never one to rely on rumors and gossip, yesterday afternoon she'd contacted her friend Alex to run a background check on George and Sam.

Alex did background checks for businesses all the time in her capacity as a private investigator. Not wanting to disrupt her friend's Christmas too much, Abby told her that George was the important one, since he was dating her mother. Sam could wait. It would be interesting, though, to discover more about the handsome man leaning against the door frame.

"You look very nice." He raised one of the glasses. "All Christmas-y."

She'd dressed up in her new red sweater and her black dress slacks instead of her usual reindeer sweatshirt and old jeans because she wanted to. She even wore dress flats instead of athletic shoes. Again, because she wanted to. It certainly wasn't for him, although he did look attractive in a dark red shirt with a green Grinch tie. His black trousers seemed loose, as if only the narrow black belt kept them from falling off his slim hips. She wondered if he'd recently lost weight.

"Why are you stuck back here in the kitchen?" he asked. "You should be joining in the festivities in the living room."

Heat bloomed in her cheeks, heat that had nothing to do with the temperature in the kitchen. "I'm fine in here. Lots to do."

"What can I do to help?"

"Nothing. Would you like a drink?" she offered, trying to change the subject. Then, she wanted to thunk her forehead seeing what he had in his hands.

"Got one. Actually, two." He held out one glass. "Dad fixed this, so it might be a little strong."

Wiping her hands on her apron, she came closer. After taking a sip, she gasped as whiskey burned its way down her throat. "A *little* strong? Yikes."

"Dad can be heavy-handed with the liquor." Sam chuckled. "Let me water it down for you." When she nodded, he took her glass over to the refrigerator and added water from the dispenser in the left door. "That should be better."

As he handed the glass back to her, her fingers grazed his. A spark she hadn't felt in years traveled up her hand. She almost dropped the glass. His hand cupped the bottom, and his gray eyes bore into hers for a moment, before she averted hers. The man unnerved her.

"Would you please open that window?" She pointed to the one closest to the stove. She could've done it herself, if her feet hadn't planted themselves in the floor.

After opening the window, he leaned against the island in the middle of the kitchen. "I guess we're going to be seeing each other often."

She was afraid of that. For the past six years, ever since Father died, it had been just the three of them. Now it was five. Too much, too soon. She wasn't ready for change. Besides, nobody could take Father's place.

"So I've heard," she muttered.

"You don't sound very happy." He gave her a wary look. "Don't you like my father?"

To delay answering, she took another sip. The drink went down better this time. "I never met him until early yesterday morning. If Mother is in love with him, why hasn't she introduced us?"

He thought about that. In fact, it had been one of his questions when Dad said he was in love with Flo. "Maybe she was afraid you wouldn't approve. In fact, you and I haven't been properly introduced." After setting his glass on the island counter, he held out his hand. "Sam Watson."

She, too, set down her glass then wiped her hand on her apron before clasping his. "Abigail Ten Eyck. Abby."

His big hand engulfed hers, warm, reassuring, strong. Comforting. What odd thoughts. Almost fanciful. She didn't need a strong, comforting man in her life. He still held her hand. Without making an issue, she couldn't very well tug hers away.

"It's not that I disapprove," she said. "And I want her to be happy but . . ."

"You don't know us," he finished. Still holding her hand, he led her to the doorway. "Here's to getting to know us better." He glanced up at the mistletoe. "Who's the thoughtful person who hung this?"

Without waiting for an answer, he pulled her close. *Oh, no.* He was going to kiss her. Mesmerized by his gray eyes turning as dark as storm clouds over Lake Michigan, she didn't, couldn't move.

He wrapped his arm around her waist then kissed her. "Merry Christmas."

CHAPTER FIVE

Sensing they were not alone, Abby broke away from Sam. Her cheeks burned hotter than the steam-filled kitchen.

"Mo-ther!" Bethany gasped with all the exasperation seventeen-year-olds could muster. Stunned by Sam's kiss, Abby couldn't think of anything to say. Scolding her daughter for putting up mistletoe would have embarrassed them even more than she already was.

Mother and George stood behind Bethany, both grinning widely.

George slapped Sam on the back. "Hehehe, son. Better watch out for those Ten Eyck women. Just ask me. Now, get out of the way and let me have some fun."

With a playful poke, George elbowed Sam out of the doorway and took his place. Using a move straight out of a 1940's flick, he dipped Mother over his arm and planted a steamy kiss on her. Abby hoped *she* didn't have that dopey expression on *her* face when Sam finished their kiss.

"Go, Grandma!" Bethany cheered.

Abby's emotions zoomed from embarrassed to fuming. Bethany was okay with her grandmother kissing under the mistletoe but not her mother? She would have words with her daughter when they got home. Strengthening her resolve, Abby repeated her vow not to let anything spoil their last Christmas in the house she'd grown up in.

Our last Christmas.

Dang. Tears gathered behind her eyelids. She had to get out of there before she embarrassed herself further. Ignoring her mother's giggles, Bethany's cheers, and George's antics, Abby scurried to the back door and yanked it open. Blessedly cool—make that cold—air hit her along with a spray of snow from the roof as she stepped out onto the wide back porch. She pulled the door quietly behind her.

God, what a mess. And she didn't mean the lake effect snow blanketing Far Haven and most of west Michigan. Starting last night, the winds howled off Lake Michigan until late in the morning. Though the winds had diminished, the snow kept falling. Ten inches according to the weather report that morning. More by now, eight hours later.

She wrapped her arms around her, holding in her grief. If she let the tears fall, they'd freeze on her cheeks. Tears for a house. How ridiculous. Grief for her childhood home. A tear escaped. With freezing fingers, she swiped at it.

She'd tried to convince Mother not to sell the old Victorian in Far Haven's historic district. Did her mother listen? Of course not. Did she ever listen to Abby? Yeah, right.

A blast of heat warmed her back. Someone had opened the door.

"Go back inside, Bethany. I'm fine."

"Not Bethany." The soft baritone rumbled behind her.

Sam Watson.

"Same message. Go back inside." Abby didn't bother to hide her displeasure at Sam's presence. She didn't want anyone to witness her breakdown. Hardly a real breakdown, she scoffed at herself. That would be when she sobbed uncontrollably and tears waterfalled down her cheeks, like the night after Mother's announcement. This was a minor upset.

God, she hated change.

A heavy coat landed on her shoulders. "Flo is worried about you. So is Bethany."

"I'll *bet* they're worried. More like anxious dinner will burn and ruin the holiday."

"I think the three of them will make sure it doesn't. Dad isn't too bad in the kitchen." Sam kept his hands on her shoulders over the coat, generating a different kind of heat. "Did I upset you with that kiss?"

Upset her? Heck, yeah. She liked it. More than liked it. His kiss that started out playful had turned into something more intense and awakened long-buried wanting deep inside her. A longing that embarrassed her more than Bethany's exasperation or George's teasing. What had she been thinking to succumb to a kiss under the mistletoe? By a guy she hardly knew?

Add to that his hands on her shoulders. She'd been without a man's touch for so long she'd forgotten how good it felt. Too good.

When she turned her head to tell him to leave, she realized it wasn't her coat around her shoulders. She should have known since it was so long the cuffs hung below her fingers. The rich leather felt buttery smooth against her cheek. Besides the smell of leather, she caught a hint of sandalwood and outdoors. Like a forest. Not pine but something—

"I'm sorry." Sam rubbed the tops of her shoulders, generating a long-forgotten warmth deep in her belly. "Not for kissing you, which I liked very much. I embarrassed you. And for that I am sorry."

His understanding made her feel awkward. No

man—not her father, definitely not her ex— understood her. Nor had they ever made the effort to figure her out. Then this man, this stranger, had her pegged.

"I should go back inside."

He dropped his hands. "It's beautiful out here. When Flo invited me over a few months ago, I fell in love with the gardens." He scoffed. "Me. A condo guy entranced by a garden."

Months? Abby hadn't realized how long her mother had kept George and Sam a secret. Hurt reared up inside. Hurt that Mother would keep something so important from her.

Sam continued, "When I was a kid, we vacationed on Lake Michigan. My mother's family had a cottage near Petoskey. I always thought the lake was peaceful, but I never realized how soothing a beautifully-designed garden could be."

"Mother has a green thumb." She groaned. "That is such a cliché, but it's true."

Mother's pride and joy had always been her flower beds. As a Master Gardener, she'd arranged the plants so something bloomed from early spring to late fall. Although she had a lawn-mowing service, Mother never let anyone touch her garden. The new owners would probably destroy it. Too much work. Insider her chest, something twisted. New owners. Someone else sleeping in her bedroom, eating in the breakfast nook, reading books in her turret.

With her arms wrapped around her waist, she stifled the pain.

"I can't believe she wants to sell this." Her voice thickened as she waved her hand to include the large backyard, the gazebo where she and her girlfriends partied, quietly, late into the night. The huge garage at one time had been a carriage house, large enough for two coaches and four horses to pull them. Now the garage held her mother's red Mustang convertible, the outdoor furniture, and Father's workshop, with room to spare. Beyond the garage, she could see the lake—the storm clouds breaking up and sunlight trying to pop through.

"That bothers you, a lot. Her wanting to sell." He stated the obvious. "She's starting a new life, with my father. I think that bothers you more."

Again, with the insight into her feelings. Was this man psychic?

She nodded. "She kept saying the house and property were too much to keep up. But now I realize that isn't the only reason. I didn't know about your father until the two of them were arrested."

Sam laughed. The rumble of his amusement behind her made her want to laugh with him. With the exception of her close friends, she didn't laugh often. In fact, they often chided her that she worked too hard and didn't laugh enough. But it was easy to laugh with Sam. Too easy. She didn't like the feelings generated by this man. Holding her, kissing her. Fifteen years of going without. Fifteen years longing for more.

She'd thought Ferret Face had killed that part of her. Now, she feared Sam revived it.

From his father's stories, Sam knew more about Abby than she probably wanted. Intense, driven. Abby had inherited much from her conservative, workaholic father. Sam knew all about being driven. Though his ulcers had healed and his blood pressure lowered back into the safe range, he remembered the consequences of his former life. That life had almost killed him.

Other than Abby's brief marriage against her father's wishes, he learned, she'd toed the straight and narrow, running her gift shop as if it were a Fortune 500 company—the same approach she applied to cooking Christmas dinner. The woman rarely laughed. He'd hoped a quick kiss under the mistletoe would help her ease up, maybe even make her laugh. Instead, he'd made things worse.

When his lips had lightly grazed hers, she'd responded, clutching his shoulders tightly, which led to his deepening the kiss. Big mistake. He'd frightened her.

"Do you feel your mother is betraying your father by loving mine?"

She started beneath his hands. He'd kept them on her shoulders when he wanted to wrap them around her. He'd never fallen so hard for a woman. Especially a woman he'd seen only three times before. Or maybe learning about her from his dad and her mother over the past couple of months had drawn him in. Meeting her at the jail, wearing that sleepshirt over faded jeans and her bare feet stuffed into flannel-lined clogs, had clinched it.

Or maybe it had been her wildly-tousled sable-brown hair that night. Not the usual tightly-bound bun or French twist she wore at the store. In the wee hours of yesterday morning, she looked like she'd just gotten out of bed—which she probably had—after a wild night of passion. Which he assumed she hadn't. That was something he wanted to see someday. And he wanted to be the one who messed up her hair.

He wanted to yank of the clasp confining her hair at the base of her neck and run his fingers through those silky strands. For sure, that would make her run away.

"Not really."

Sam's wandering thoughts made him forget what he'd asked.

"Father has been gone for almost six years." She turned beneath his hands to look up at him, surprise and sadness in her deep blue eyes that reminded him of Lake Michigan on a summer day, like when he'd vacationed there as a child.

"Everything has happened too fast," she went on. "Mother never told me she was dating. I guess she wasn't playing bingo all those nights." She ended with a bitter laugh.

Sam had to chuckle. "Nope. Unless *playing bingo* is a euphemism for the horizontal mambo."

"Oh, please." She shivered. "That's an image I could do without. Thanks for the coat. We should go in. You must be freezing, and I need to check on Christmas dinner, or we're all be going to Denny's or the Chinese Buffet."

"Hang on a minute." He stopped her from opening the back door. "My father loves your mother very much. I'm glad he found someone who makes him happy. Mom's Alzheimer's took a lot out of him. Out of both of us."

A stricken look crossed her face. She reached up to touch his cheek, but at the last moment stopped. "I am so sorry. I didn't know about your mother."

Sam captured her hand. Not that he didn't want her to touch him or stroke his jaw. Hell, he desperately wanted it, needed it. But he didn't want to see regret in her eyes. "How would you? We hardly know each other. I'd like to remedy that." He searched her gorgeous blue eyes.

When she jerked her hand away and averted his eyes, disappointment raced through him. He had a long way to go before she stopped being skittish around him. Before she trusted him.

Damn that ex-husband.

Warmth and a delicious combination of cooking aromas greeted them as they went inside. At the stove, George turned from stirring something and raised his eyebrow at Sam. "Everything okay?"

"Abby needed some fresh air," he said before she spoke. "She's been working in the kitchen too long, while we were all goofing off."

"Oh, Mom." A guilty look crossed Bethany's face. "I'm sorry I didn't come out and help you."

When Flo chimed in, Abby snorted. "You both offered, but you know me. I like being in charge."

And that was the crux of her problems. Sam knew exactly how that felt. An obligation to prevent her from learning the hard way filled him with purpose. Yes, if he could save one person, save Abby, from experiencing pain the way he had, his life would have meaning again. He needed to save her from the pain that had doubled him over and sent him running into the john attached to his office. Pain that caused his sweat glands to work overtime. Pain that killed his appetite until his weight loss was so obvious, even self-absorbed Nadine noticed. Nobody should have to endure that. Or blood pressure that shot up into the danger zone. His doctor had warned him repeatedly that if the ulcers didn't kill him, a stroke would. It almost had.

"Now, where are we?" Abby lifted lids on pots and gave the turkey—at least a twenty-five pounder—sitting on the counter next to the stove a long look. "I take it Tom is done?"

"Yep," Bethany said. "The little thermometer thingee popped up right after you left. I scooped out the stuffing, and Grandma turned on the potatoes. Mr. Watson used the meat thermometer to check the turkey and said it had to rest before carving."

"George, dear. You can call me George."

"I know." With a giggle, she nodded. "George."

In the small kitchen, the five of them kept running into each other. Still, they managed to bring all the food, enough for three times as many people, out to the formal dining room. A cheery red tablecloth covered with white lace held five place settings of Spode Christmas Tree dishes. Sam swallowed hard. His mother had the same set. He wondered if his dad experienced the same sense of loss as he did seeing the dishes. Even though, physically Mom had been gone for four years, she'd mentally left them two years before that—one of the reasons Alzheimer's was called the long good-bye.

After he set the large turkey-laden platter in the middle of the table, he glanced at his dad. Unshed tears swam in George's eyes. He remembered.

Sam had taken a step toward his dad, when Flo bustled out with a crystal cut-glass bowl of cranberry salad in one hand and a pale green fluffy one in her other. "George, please take this before I drop it." She held out the glass bowl of green fluff, which he promptly took. "Wait until you taste my Watergate Salad. It is so refreshing."

"Watergate? As in Nixon's Watergate?" George exclaimed.

To which Flo replied, "Yes, silly. It's a salad they serve at the hotel and has nothing to do with Nixon and his gang of crooks."

"Coming through. Hot gravy." Bethany set a white lid-covered spouted bowl on the table. "We read about President Nixon and Watergate in history class. I didn't know that's what your green fluff is really called, Gram."

"Well, it is. Sit, everybody."

"C'mon, Mom," Bethany called out. "We only

need the rolls."

Abby came in with a holiday towel-covered red basket. "I'm coming, I'm coming."

"Oh, my goodness." George shook his head. "You ladies outdid yourselves. What a feast."

A feast was right. So different from the last four Christmases when he and Dad had grazed on an assortment of appetizers all day rather than make a traditional meal. The holidays always hit them hard, especially with Mom dying three days before.

Sam was surprised that Dad had accepted Flo's invitation to dinner. He'd never accepted Aunt Grace's invitations. His mother's older sister tried to include them in her family's celebrations. During Thanksgiving, children, spouses, grandchildren, and a great-grandson filled Aunt Grace's condo to bursting. Christmas was different. She didn't need two mopey bachelors ruining Christmas for her large extended brood. This year, things had changed, for the better. Dad had seemed eager to join Flo and her girls, as she called them. Sam, too, appreciated her efforts to make this the best Christmas he and Dad had in years.

As soon as everyone sat, Flo insisted they hold hands for the blessing. Sam clasped Abby's while she held George's, at the foot of the table. Sam liked that she sat between them, as if she belonged in their family. If his dad had his way, she would. Soon.

"Heavenly Father, bless my loved ones gathered together at this table." Flo gave George a big smile, before sharing it with the rest of them. "Two families gathered together as one. May this be the beginning of a family tradition. Bless this food and the hands that prepared it. Amen."

Everyone echoed the "Amen." For several

moments, as the food was passed, nobody spoke. Then, Abby said, "Mother, what did you mean about a family tradition?"

"We'll be seeing a lot more of George and Sam."

CHAPTER SIX

Dinner passed in a flurry of excitement for Bethany and Flo, with George grinning happily. But Sam watched Abby who'd pasted a smile on her lips. A smile that didn't reach her eyes, clouded in worry. Though she made a production out of moving the food around on her plate, he knew she'd eaten little.

When it looked like everyone was finished, she started to get up. Bethany promptly announced, "Mom, sit. You cooked. Grandma and I agreed we'll clean up."

"Me, too," George added. "I'll help, if you ladies don't mind."

As the others grabbed bowls and platters, Sam held up the bottle of wine to Abby. "There's a little left. Would you like to finish it?"

She glanced around at the empty table, as if suddenly realizing they were alone. "Sure. I could use something stronger, though."

"You aren't pleased." He poured the last of the wine into her glass.

"About them clearing the table? I appreciate their help."

He knew she used that as an excuse to avoid the real issue. He decided to push it. "I meant your mother's announcement."

She gulped down the golden liquid. "Surprised. Maybe. Not really." She shrugged. "I figured your dad would be around a lot more now."

When her cell chirped a text pending, she

pulled her phone out of her slacks' pocket.

"I'll get you a stronger drink." As Sam scooted behind her, he glanced down at her phone.

> *George Watson checks out A-OK. No worries for your mom. Report to follow via email. Merry Christmas! – Alex O'Hara & Palzetti Investigators.*

"What is that?" He pointed. "You had my dad investigated?"

"Shh."

"Don't you shush me." Sam felt his blood pressure escalate. *She sicced an investigator on Dad?* The duplicity of his thoughts hit him but didn't lessen his anger that she'd hired a PI to investigate his dad.

"Let's go outside." She rose and grabbed his hand. "Sam and I are going for a walk," she called out to those in the kitchen before hauling him to the front closet. "Please don't make a scene," she whispered.

She tossed their outdoor wear on the bench then sat to pull on boots.

"Me? Make a scene?" Tossing their coats, hats, scarves, and gloves on the floor, he made room on the bench to put his own boots on. "Why would you think that?"

When she rolled her eyes at him, he knew his sarcasm had gotten through. Bundled up like kids at recess, they headed outside. The snow had stopped and the sun, though low in the sky, made the trees sparkle. The inviting scene was quickly lost on him as he thought about what she'd done.

"You had my dad investigated," he repeated as he strode down the block. Neighbors or snow-removal services had cleared most of the sidewalks. When he realized she had to scurry to keep up, he slowed down.

"Of course, I did. When I got home from the jail yesterday morning, all I knew about your father was that he and my mother had been arrested and were spending Christmas in jail. At the time, I thought your father led my mother astray." When he sputtered at the unfair accusation, she added, "Note, I said *thought* he'd led her astray. I know better now. Anyway, I called my friend Alex who is a PI. Can you blame me? I had to protect my mother. Father left her comfortably well off. For all I knew, your father could be a gold digger."

Sam threw his head back and laughed. If she only knew. "Dad doesn't look like much, but he's pretty well off himself."

More than well off. With several patents to his name and a smart attorney, Dad was a millionaire several times over. Thanks in part to Sam's smart investing, Dad had weathered the disaster of two thousand eight and nine.

They strolled in comfortable silence, passing stately Victorian houses similar to Flo's.

"So, this is Far Haven's historic district," he broke the silence.

"*Unofficial* historic district. Father tried to organize a commission to oversee restoration and preservation, to make sure the houses were properly restored and maintained."

"From the state of some of the houses, I see he wasn't successful. What happened?"

She laughed. "People here are pretty independent. They don't like people or committees telling them what to do with their homes. So, no historic committee. But it would be good if houses were kept up and looked like they did a hundred years ago."

"I can see both sides. Nobody likes being told what to do with their property. At the same time, some of the houses here could be in better condition. Flo's house is in fine shape. I can tell a lot of work was put in to maintain it."

They rounded a corner so they were on a street parallel to Flo's house, though a couple of blocks east.

"Father insisted. The house has been in Mother's family since 1901. That's what's so damn, I mean dang hard. The house is a treasure. Our family's treasure. I don't understand why Mother wants to let it go."

Sam wasn't sure how to ask. Finally, he just did. "Please don't think I'm prying into your finances, but why don't you take over?"

"I wish I could. I can manage the taxes on my own home because of the shop. Over fifty percent of the building is a business expense. I could barely afford the taxes on Mother's house. Add in utilities and maintenance . . ." She blew out a frosty breath. "I can't. I just can't, as much as I want to."

Sam could see how that affected her. Though she kept a tight rein on her emotions, her eyes conveyed how hard she found it to do nothing while her family home passed out of her family.

They continued in silence for a while to the end of the block then around the corner. Finally, he said, "How far are we planning to walk?"

"Around the next corner. Too much food." Over her winter jacket, she patted her slim belly. "Mother always went overboard when Father was with us. Then we ate leftovers for a week."

Sam laughed. His mother used to do that. He thought about all those meals. How he and Dad used to grouse about the leftovers. He'd give anything now to have his mother back. He didn't often become sentimental. Must be the day. Mom had always made Christmas fun. For the past four years, it had been a day to get through. He'd made a point of coming home each year to be with his dad. Today was the first time he'd seen George happy again.

"In all fairness, I should tell you I did the same." Despite the cold, his ears burned.

At Sam's announcement, Abby stopped in front of her mother's house. "What do you mean you did the same? The same what?"

"When Dad started dating Flo, I had her investigated. Your friend Alex is quite thorough."

"You what?"

"You heard me." He cleared his throat. "I hired Alex O'Hara, too. She does a good job."

"You hired Alex?" Her voice held a tinge of anger. "To check out my mother?" She stooped to retie the boot laces—although he couldn't figure out why since they were going inside. "I agree she is very efficient."

Abby rose then scooted away. She let loose a round, white ball. Smack into his chest.

For a moment, he stood still near the snow-covered lawn, a patch of white decorating his leather jacket. "You know this means war."

With an evil laugh, he grabbed a handful of snow and packed it well. As he threw it, she dodged. He anticipated her move, and his aim wasn't that far off. The snowball clipped her shoulder.

"Bring it on." She fired another ball and got his ear, before dodging to the left to avoid his next throw.

They flung a barrage of snowballs at each other. After her last throw that narrowly missed a vulnerable part of his anatomy, he lunged for her and brought her down on the lawn. Her fall was well cushioned by the snow.

"You will pay for that last one," he said in a falsetto. "I plan to have children someday."

Lying on the snow-covered lawn, she looked lovely, kissable . . . until she dumped a handful of cold stuff down the back of his neck.

"Someday? You'd better hurry. *Someday* is about to pass you up. Ooh," she shrieked as his handful of snow went down the V-neck of her holiday sweater.

With strength that surprised him, she managed to roll him over then sat astride him. "Did you say war? You ain't seen nothing yet, mister." With a girlish giggle, she rubbed a handful of snow in his face.

"What are you two doing?" Flo stood on the front porch, hands on her hips. "Get up before someone sees you acting like children. What will the neighbors say?"

Abby scrambled to her feet then reached down to help him up. "Oh my yes." She pursed her lips. "What *will* the neighbors say?"

When he clasped her hand, he noticed the twinkle in her eyes. "Can't have that." He scooped her up in a fireman carry and headed for the backyard.

"You two behave yourselves," Flo called out.

The last thing Sam saw over his shoulder was George pulling Flo back into the house. "Leave them alone, sweetheart. Can't you see they're having fun?"

As Sam rounded the corner of the garage, Abby pounded on his back. "You'd better let me down, Sam Watson, or you'll be sorry."

"Promises, promises." He hadn't had a good snowball fight in years. In fact, he couldn't remember how long it had been since he'd had a good laugh.

With all her struggling, Abby's jacket had pulled up as well as her sweater, exposing a delicious strip of pink skin. He couldn't resist. Using his teeth to remove a glove, he scooped some snow off the back of her jacket and, oh so carefully, sprinkled it along that strip.

She shrieked and wiggled so much, he had to drop her . . . in a big snowbank behind the garage. This time, he straddled her. "Give up?"

"'Never give up, never surrender,'" she quoted a sci-fi movie spoof.

He held a handful of snow over her face. "Are you sure?"

"Go ahead." She stiffened. "I dare you."

"Double dare?"

In anticipation of him smushing snow over her face, she braced herself. "Double dog dare."

"C'mon, Abby. I don't want to do this. Say uncle."

"Never. Ten Eycks never give up. Or in. We never cry uncle. We make war." While she protested, he could see her hands gathering snow.

Before she could throw it, he stretched out on top of her. "I'd rather kiss than make war."

He lowered his head, making sure his lips hovered over hers. "What do you say? Kiss or war?"

Her eyes darkened, not in anger. In anticipation. She wanted that kiss. *Thank God.* He brushed his lips against hers. A deep sigh ran through her as she raised her arms to loop them around his neck. *Oh, yeah.* Her lips softened, drawing him in. Much better.

Something wet and cold was shoved down the back of his neck. With a yelp, he scrambled off her. She lay in the snow mound, laughing, as he sat up and shook off the snow.

"You are a menace," He groused. "A sneaky menace."

"Poor baby." She got to her feet. "Want some help getting the snow out?"

He checked her hands. "I'd rather have another kiss." When she hesitated, he added, "Only a kiss, Abby."

After hesitating for another moment, she said, "I'm not sure if I'm ready for more than that."

"I can wait until you are."

Looking out the kitchen window, George turned to Flo. "They're kissing again."

"Wonderful." Flo leaned against him.

"Gross," Bethany said. "They're too old for that stuff."

George and Flo just laughed. "Never too old."

CHAPTER SEVEN

"Mother, I can't believe you kissed him."
Bethany's outrage began as soon as they entered
the van.

Abby let a grin escape. What a kiss!

"And you were playing in the snow!" More
disapproval as they pulled out of Mother's driveway
onto the street.

"We were having fun. You know about fun."
She glanced over at her daughter whose mouth was
twisted in a mutinous expression.

"You were acting like children."

"Oh, give it a rest. Everybody's allowed to play
on Christmas. Did you like the necklace George
gave you?" Abby hoped that would divert Bethany's
attention.

"Yeah. It was nice. I can't believe he knew I
play the clarinet."

The necklace, a tiny black clarinet on a silver
chain, had been the perfect gift. Bethany had even
thrown her arms around George's neck and kissed
him on the cheek while Mother beamed in
approval. Abby's gift had been a personalized
ornament—a chef's hat with her name and the year.
As he said, it would remind her of the delicious
meal she'd prepared, for which he and Sam were
grateful.

Though she hadn't expected to exchange gifts—
having only met the previous day—she and Bethany
had come prepared. They'd raided her shop early
that morning. For Sam, Bethany had found a

carpenter's tools ornament. George had been harder. Neither knew much about him. Did he like to fish? Play golf? Her store carried memorabilia for any sport. After searching for anything that would trigger a response, she broke down and called her mother. When she learned he enjoyed fiddling with things, Abby knew the perfect gift. He seemed pleased with the metal brain-teaser puzzle.

"George, I mean Mr. Watson, is nice," Bethany said. "He makes Gram happy. Did you see how much she smiled?"

Abby had to admit Bethany was right. Mother did smile more, and she had a bounce to her step that Abby had never seen. Mother certainly hadn't been *bouncy* when Father was alive. "I'm glad she's happy."

"You don't sound convinced."

Leave it to her daughter to pick up on nuances of speech.

She sighed. "Too many changes."

Bethany shifted in her seat to look at Abby. "Life is full of changes. It's how we deal with change that counts."

"My daughter, the philosopher."

Bethany laughed. "I read that on a calendar."

The short trip home ended at the sidedoor to the shop. Bethany stopped her from turning off the van. "Mom, we need to talk."

Ominous words.

"We can talk upstairs."

"No. You'll get all busy putting away the leftover food, and then you'll be on your computer tallying sales and balancing the books."

Abby was stunned at Bethany's description. She hated to admit it, but her daughter was right. That's exactly what she would've done when they went upstairs.

"Okay." Following Bethany's motion, she unlatched her seatbelt and half-turned to face her daughter. "What do we need to talk about?"

"Besides Gram and George? How about her selling the house? I know you're upset. I am, too."

That surprised Abby. Bethany hadn't said a word about Mother selling her house. Not since she'd found out at the jail.

"I've been thinking about it, Mom." She clasped Abby's hand. "A lot. I love that big, old house. I remember playing in the turret when I was little."

When Abby returned home after the divorce, she and Bethany had lived with her parents until she got back on her feet. It had taken more years than Abby had expected, she'd had to wait until the gift shop made enough money to support the two of them.

"I have a lot of good memories," Bethany went on. "I'm sure you have a lot, too."

She did. More good than bad, but the bad stood out. Her father's "I told you so" about Ferret Face, Mother's frequent disapproval of Abby's parenting methods. Father's haranguing her about opening a gift shop instead of using her business degree at one of the major employers either in town or in Grand Rapids. Too risky, he'd said, followed by statistics on the rate of new business failures.

If she could erase those bad memories, like words from a chalkboard, she would. Instead, they stuck as if engraved in her mind.

". . . with George?"

While she'd gone off into memories, Bethany had been talking. *Dang it.*

"I'm sorry, sweetie. I didn't catch that last part."

"Tripping down Memory Lane?" She laughed, obviously not offended by Abby's inattention, since she did it often enough.

Still, heat filled her face. "Sorry. Thinking about Grandpa."

"I know Christmas is hard on you and Grandma without him. But, Mom, she's found George, and he loves her. It's so obvious and kinda cute. She giggles. I never heard Grandma giggle before."

Abby hadn't, either.

"We should be happy for her."

"I am, sweetie. I am." Maybe if she said it enough, she would believe it. She wanted her mother to be happy—the same way she wanted Bethany to be happy.

"Anyway, about the house." Bethany took a deep breath. "Can't we buy it?" Without waiting for Abby, she went on. "I want to live there. I want my children to play there. I want the house to stay in our family. We have to buy it. Please, Mom?"

Her passionate plea knifed through Abby's heart. Everything Bethany said echoed her own thoughts. Watching her grandchildren race around corners, sliding on sock-clad feet across the foyer— the way she and Bethany did when Father wasn't home.

But she had to cut off Bethany's pipedream. "We can't, sweetie. I wish we could."

After Abby and Bethany went home, Dad said he and Flo had some things to talk about. Sam made himself scarce by wandering out to the garage, by way of a breezeway that connected it to the house. There he found a workshop to die for. And a treasure trove of tools. Flo's former husband had every woodworking tool available, in drawers or hanging on pegboards on the wall. Fine chisels, lathes, sanders, scroll and band saws. Scribes, gouges, sharpening stones. A woodworker's dream.

Despite the cold outside, the garage was so warm he took off his jacket. He found the source, an overhead infrared heater. No wonder the tools seemed to be in good condition, though they hadn't been used in several years. He was impressed with the precision instruments and the care with which the tools had been maintained. He'd been so thoroughly engrossed in the workshop he was surprised with Dad came in and said he was ready to leave.

"Pretty impressive, right?" Dad asked.

Sam slipped his jacket on. "Amazing. What will happen to all this when the house is sold?"

"I imagine Flo will have an estate sale."

That made sense. He hoped she would get a fair price, especially for the tools. Abby's father had amassed a fine collection of tools, implements any woodworker would give his eyeteeth for. Maybe he could help her by ensuring she valued the tools appropriately.

Their good-byes in the foyer lasted longer than Sam expected. After thanks for the meal and gifts, Flo piled their arms with packages of left-overs. They wouldn't have to cook for the next few days. She hugged him, and even though she lacked the height, she stood on tiptoes to kiss his cheek.

"I'm so glad you came. Don't be a stranger. You don't have to wait for your father to bring you over." She winked.

After thanking her again, he eased his way outside to give them privacy for their good-byes. At his SUV, he waited for his dad. Looking at the house, still lit up in welcome, he could understand Abby's sorrow at the house passing out of her family. That was a family home. One meant for children and grandchildren. Not a lone, old woman.

But, as soon as they entered Sam's SUV, the interrogation began.

"So. You and Abby?" Dad didn't even wait until Sam started the engine.

"What do you mean?" He stalled.

"You know exactly what I mean. You kissed her. Twice."

Sam grinned. More than twice. Dad obviously hadn't seen him kiss her on the back porch.

"Yeah. I did."

"Don't trifle with her. She's fragile." Dad's protectiveness surprised Sam.

"Figured that out all by myself, Dad. Her ex did a number on her." He'd like to punch the guy's lights out for the damage he'd done to Abby.

"He sure did. And I don't want you adding to her pain."

Sam didn't want that, either. "I'm going slow."

"Slow? Is that what you call cavorting in the snow in Flo's front yard?"

"Cavorting? Is that your word for the day?" He grinned over at his father to let him know he was teasing. Even since Sam had shown him the app store for his cell phone, Dad found all kinds of freebie sites. One of which was a word-of-the-day.

"Nah. Today's word was capricious, which means impulsive, which I don't want you to be with Abby."

"Smart ass. And I am not capricious."

During the rest of the drive silence stretched between them, both lost in thought. Sam pulled up to the garage attached to Dad's condo. With Sam's woodworking shop on one side of the garage, there wasn't room for two vehicles. He thought enviously of that huge unused workshop at Flo's.

"I can't believe we brought home all this food,"

Dad exclaimed as he made room in the refrigerator. "That was real nice of Abby and Beth to package it up for us."

"She lets you call her Beth?"

Abby had been particular about calling her daughter by her whole name. That seemed odd to Sam since she went by a nickname.

Dad grinned. "She said she only lets her friends call her Beth. Guess I'm a friend now. She's a sweet kid."

"That necklace was a big hit." Sam leaned against the small kitchen island.

Dad turned out the kitchen light and headed for his recliner in the Great Room. "I can be thoughtful, you know."

"You're always thoughtful." Sam followed but didn't sit. "I haven't said it enough, but thanks for letting me stay here."

"Not a problem. You were pretty sick when you came out from New York."

That had been a bad time. Sick didn't cover it. He'd lost his job, his girl, and nearly his life. Leaving not just his position with the investment firm after ten highly successful years, but also his career, had been one of the hardest decisions in his life. Hard but necessary. He couldn't go back to that rat race.

Nadine hadn't liked that one bit.

Income, not as important to him as it was for her, led to their parting. He hadn't realized what a mercenary she was. Status was more important than his health. To her. When she discovered his plan for the future, it had been adios, sayonara, and good-bye.

Good riddance.

He said that now. Then, devastated didn't come close to describing his feelings. Talk about kicking a guy when he's down. Better that they parted before they married, which had been part of *her* future plan. She'd made plans he hadn't considered all the time they'd been together. Plans he had no idea about.

While Sam was in the hospital, Dad had flown in from Michigan—even though Sam had told him not to. After his discharge, George brought Sam back to his penthouse apartment and stayed until he could walk farther than from the living room to his bedroom without stopping. When Dad offered to bring him back to Michigan, Sam had hesitated. Giving up all he'd worked for, the trappings of success, had kept him up for several nights.

Getting away from New York City was a decision he didn't regret. But he couldn't stay with Dad forever. Before heading off to his room, the room Dad had planned for a study, Sam paused.

"So. You and Flo? When are you two getting married?"

While he and Dad got along fine, newly-weds needed their own space. A pushing-forty son would be as welcome as weeds in Flo's garden.

Dad sputtered, got red in the face, and harrumphed a few times. "Haven't asked her yet."

"What are you waiting for, old man?"

Dropping the recliner's footrest with a thump, Dad stiffened. "Who you calling an old man? I could take you down with one hand behind my back."

Chuckling, Sam patted his dad on the shoulder. "You might be right about that."

Though he raised the footrest again, Dad glanced up at him with a concerned look. "You doing okay now? Considering how you *cavorted* this afternoon, I'm surprised you didn't need a nap." The worry in his eyes turned to mirth.

Sam yawned deliberately. "Yeah, guess I'd better hit the sack early. I mean, all that cavorting wiped me right out." He headed around the corner toward his bedroom.

"Samuel? You are feeling better, aren't you?"

He turned back. "Yes. I am. That doc yours sent me to gave me a clean bill of health. Said if I watched what I eat, exercised regularly, and stayed away from alcohol, caffeine, and stress, I could live to be an old man. Like you."

"Get outta here." Dad picked up the remote but didn't turn on the television. "Flo and I need to talk about some things before we get serious about marriage."

"I assumed when she mentioned selling her house you two *are* serious."

"That took me by surprise. I had no idea she was thinking about it until she told me she'd talked to her friend, the real estate agent. She said she'd been thinking about it for a long time. In fact, before we even reconnected."

"Hang on. Reconnected?" Sam came back to the living room and sat on the sofa. "You and Flo knew each other before?" When Dad nodded, an ugly thought raced through his mind. "While you were with Mom?"

Again, Dad dropped the footrest with a bang. "Absolutely not. I should wash your mouth out for even thinking such a thing."

Sam held up his hands. "Whoa there. I'm sorry. I shouldn't have said that."

"Damn right, you shouldn't have. I was faithful to your mother. Even when her mind was gone, and she didn't remember who I was."

Guilt snaked through Sam. In the past, he never blurted out thoughts. Control, tight control, had been a way of life for him for years. One of the things the therapist had said was not to keep things bottled up inside so they festered. But he'd crossed the line when he asked his father if he'd been faithful.

"Again, I'm sorry, Dad." He blew out a breath. "When did you and Flo meet? Originally?"

"Weren't you going to bed?"

For a few moments, Sam debated staying and asking more about Flo. But when the television came on, he knew Dad was done talking. At least for the night.

He lay in bed, his mind hopscotching from one thing to another. Two women featured prominently in his thoughts. Florence Ten Eyck and her daughter.

Abby lay awake long into the night.

Sam Watson confused her. His kisses made her *feel*. Feel things she hadn't felt in ages. He brought her senses alive. Not just the surge of lust when he kissed her. He made her feel like a teen on the cusp of womanhood, when hormones raged.

She got all hot and bothered just thinking about him. She never played in the snow. Hadn't since she met Ferret Face. God, she'd called him that for so long, she almost didn't remember his name. At least, she never said it out loud. Neither of her parents—and certainly not Bethany—knew the whole story. For her daughter's sake, she kept her animosity toward him hidden. She never wanted Bethany to believe her father didn't want her.

Abby felt her usual anger at the man rise up inside her and tried to tamp it down.

Think about something else.

Like what?

Christmas dinner. *Oh, shoot.* She hadn't

responded to Alex. When she grabbed her cell off the charger, she noticed the time. Dear God, it was after midnight. She couldn't call or text Alex now. She'd be in bed with that hunky Nick Palzetti. Lucky Alex.

Abby typed a quick reminder to text her friend and thank her for finding out about George Watson. Grateful that Alex had set her mind at ease, she typed another note to invite Alex out for dinner next week.

She needed to get some sleep.

Instead, you thought about how lucky Alex was to have reconnected with her teenage crush. Every girl in their high school had a crush on Nick, including Abby who was three years older. Oh, yeah. That guy with his swaggering walk made them all drool.

And now Alex had him.

Abby envied her. She'd resigned herself to forgoing that part of life. After Ferret—Kevin— destroyed her confidence, Abby let her feelings for a man dry up. She didn't need that grief in her life. She had Bethany, for whom she was grateful. She had her mother, who drove her crazy. And she had friends. What more did she need?

A man's arms around her.

A man's kisses.

A man's lovemaking.

Abigail Louise, get your mind off that subject.

Morning came too early. Instead of her alarm, her cell woke her up. *Better not be the police again.*

"Mom?" Bethany? Why was she calling? "Sorry to wake you, but I need some help down here."

Abby couldn't believe the clock. Ten thirty-five.

She flew to the bathroom, threw on some clothes, scooped her hair into the claws, and dashed downstairs.

Of all days to be late. Her day-after-Christmas sale was in full swing. Bethany was trying to answer clamoring questions and ring up sales. She gave Abby a look of relief and directed those with questions to her.

Dottie Matthews, sans children, rushed up, a basket on her arm. The collapsible baskets had been Bethany's idea. People might buy more if they didn't have to balance items in their hands. She was right, as evidenced by Dottie's overflowing basket.

"I can't believe your sale," Dottie enthused. "I'm getting gifts for birthdays and next Christmas."

Abby smiled. Before annual inventory, she wanted to sell off as much as she could. Her main objective, though, was to see what were her bestsellers. Not that she couldn't guess. Having the figures would not only confirm her conjecture but help her with ordering. The sale would also clear out the deadwood, those items that had been around too long. At the end of the week, she would see what was left and mark them down further, then remind herself not to re-order as many, or any.

The bell rang signifying another customer. Sam Watson. Remembering his kiss, Abby couldn't believe the rush of heat that went through her. She gave him a quick smile. When he saw she was busy, he nodded and turned to look at the miniatures.

Dottie leaned close. "You know him? Mr. Tall, Dark, and OMG-Handsome? Yowza. Get me a fan."

Abby let her go on in the same vein, agreeing whole-heartedly.

"Aren't you going to say anything?" Dottie came up for air.

"Why? You're doing great all by yourself?"

"You blushed when he came in." Her friend eyed her with suspicion. "Not that I don't blame you. What a hottie."

"And you're a married woman."

"Hey, I may be married, but I'm not dead. He is one fine-looking man. How do you know him?"

Abby sighed. "His father is dating my mother."

"You're kidding me." Dottie's eyes widened. "Give me the deets."

"Excuse me. Can you help me?" A customer interrupted. She held out a T-shirt, one found in most gift shops in Michigan, *Great Lakes. No salt. No Sharks.* "Do you have this in a 3X?"

"I'm not sure, but let me check." She nodded to Dottie. "See you later."

"The deets, girl." Dottie's eyes warned. "Later."

An hour and thirty customers later, Abby looked around the empty shop. At some point, Sam had left. Grateful and disappointed at the same time, she heaved a sigh. "We did good, didn't we, sweetie?"

Bethany smiled. "Everybody loves a bargain."

"Thanks for letting me sleep in. Did you turn off my alarm?"

"You looked so peaceful. Yesterday was a hard day for you. What with cooking and playing with Sam." She grinned.

Abby ignored the last. "You shouldn't have turned off my alarm."

"I didn't realize how crazy it gets the day after Christmas."

This was the first year Bethany worked longer hours at the shop, especially working during the holidays. Between that and waitressing at the restaurant, she was stretching herself thin. Before Abby could say anything, the bell over the door rang. She groaned, until she turned around and saw Sam carrying in a large bag from Main Street Café. As he came closer, the aromas made her mouth water and her stomach growl.

"I figured you two could use some nourishment." He set the bag on the counter. "Why don't you both go in the back room and put your feet up for a while. I'll stand guard out here." He grinned.

Bethany raced around the counter and threw herself into his arms. "You are a lifesaver." She gave him a quick peck on the cheek before grabbing the bag off the counter and heading to the back room.

"Do I get a kiss from you, too?" he said to Abby softly.

"I, uh . . ." Heat rushed into her face. She leaned over the counter and gave him a quick kiss. One shorter than Bethany's. "Thanks. That was very thoughtful of you. I was just going to send her upstairs to eat."

He gave her a knowing look. "And I'll bet you wouldn't have gotten anything for yourself."

"Mo-om, come on, before it gets cold."

Saved from answering Sam, Abby shrugged. "Are you sure you're okay out here?"

"Go." He shooed her away. "Before more customers come."

That night, Abby soaked in the tub. Her legs ached. In fact, her whole body ached. Business had been brisk before Christmas. Today was a killer. She'd had sales before, but nothing like this. What was it about a sale that made people so crazy? She recognized most of the customers, but some were strangers. Visitors to families or just to the area.

Whatever the reason, she was grateful. And more grateful to Sam for his thoughtfulness.

The short respite did her and Bethany good. And the food, heavenly. Just what they needed, especially Abby who hadn't had breakfast.

What was it about that man that made her blush like a schoolgirl and think naughty thoughts? Like the thoughts racing through her mind at that moment. She wondered what he looked like without his shirt?

A knock on the door brought her out of her reverie. "Are you going to be much longer, Mom? I can go downstairs if you are."

Abby sat up, splashing water over the edge. "I can pull the curtain. You don't need to go downstairs"

A one-bathroom apartment often presented challenges, but they'd managed. As Bethany washed her hands, she said, "That sure was nice of Sam to bring us lunch."

"It was."

"He's a nice guy."

"He is."

"I'm, uh, sorry I gave you a hard time yesterday."

Abby peeked around the curtain. Bethany sat on the closed toilet lid.

"I was surprised that you kissed a man you just met. Didn't you tell me to wait until the third date?" She smirked. "I guess it's different with *old* people. You don't have much time, so you have to get it on right away."

"*Old* people?" Abby sputtered trying to think of a snappy comeback. "I'll have you know, young lady, I am not old. And I'm not dead," she quoted her friend Dottie.

"Good thing. I've been worried about you being alone when I go off to college."

Amazed to hear her daughter voice one of her fears, Abby did worry about being alone when her chick flew the nest. Yet, she was so proud of her daughter for earning acceptance to the University of Michigan.

"Mom? Did you fall asleep in there?"

"No. Just thinking about you and college."

Bethany was silent for several moments. "Would you rather I live at home and commute to Grand Valley State? Tuition is cheaper, and we wouldn't have to pay for a dorm room."

"No. You will not give up the chance to go to U of M. I am so proud of you for getting accepted there. And earning a scholarship."

"Yeah. I'm kinda excited about that . . . and scared. But what a great opportunity to play in the marching band."

"Understandable. Listen, I'd better get out before I turn into a prune."

"Can I ask you something first? I mean, tell you?"

"Uh, sure."

"I want to go to court and change my name."

"What?" Abby held the edge of the curtain open to see her daughter. She had a mutinous look, similar to her grandmother's when she told Abby about selling the house.

"I'll be eighteen in March. I want to change my name to yours. He never visits or calls. No cards for my birthday. Nothing from his mother, either. They don't acknowledge me. I don't even want his name anymore."

Whoa. That was the last thing Abby expected. Bethany was right about Fer—Kevin. He used to promise to see her every weekend. Then he'd call on

Saturday afternoon to say he'd been sick. Yeah, sick with a hangover. When he did take her, he would dump her at his mother's in South Haven, disappear, only returning in time to bring her home. His mother was no prize, either. Not with her negative attitude toward Abby, the woman who rejected her son.

"I think this is a conversation we should have out of the bathroom."

With a sigh, Bethany left.

Dressed in a nightshirt, robe, and fuzzy slippers, Abby went out to the living room. Bethany sat in the wingback, her feet curled under her. She gave her mother a wary look.

"Would you like some tea?"

"You sound like Grandma. She thinks tea solves everything."

"Doesn't it?" Abby laughed. "Where do you think I learned it?"

A few minutes later, she brought mugs of tea to the living room. After settling on the sofa, she, too, curled her feet under her. "Why did you bring up your name change in the bathroom?"

"I didn't want to see your face when I told you."

Confused, Abby asked, "Why?"

"I was afraid you'd disapprove. I know you don't love him anymore, but I thought . . . I don't know what I thought." Bethany shrugged, helpless at being unable to put her thoughts into words.

"I understand where you're coming from." She did understand. "I don't disapprove. At the same time, you need to think it over. It's a big step."

"I have thought it over. I've been thinking about this for two years."

That long. Abby took a sip of tea. "It sounds like you've made up your mind."

"I have." A little defiance there.

"Do you realize the implications? I don't mean with your father and his family. I'm talking about school records, driver's license—"

"Mo-om. I went online and found out what I have to do."

I should've known she would research it. That's my girl. Thorough to a fault.

"That's what you did after the divorce. I wish you'd changed my name at the same time." She pouted.

"I couldn't without your father's permission. It's a big step. I'm proud of you for finding out the details. It is your choice. I'll help you any way I can."

Bethany leaped out of the chair and ran across the room to hug Abby who held her near-empty mug out of the way. "Thanks, Mom. You're the best."

"Remember that the next time we disagree," Abby drawled. Not that Bethany and she quarreled frequently.

"Want some more tea?" She reached for Abby's mug.

"Sure."

When she returned with fresh tea, Bethany sank into her chair. "Do you think Grandma will change hers when she marries George?"

"I suppose she will. She's pretty traditional, even though lately I'm beginning to wonder about the effect he's having on her." Like landing in jail on Christmas Eve.

A smile curved Bethany's lips. "Did you know he's a millionaire?"

Abby choked on the tea. Once she had herself under control, she said, "No I didn't know that."

"Yeah. A multi-millionaire. Gram told me."

I could've saved some money. Instead of hiring a PI, I should've asked my daughter.

"You can't always believe what someone tells you."

Good advice for the years to come. Sometimes, Bethany was too willing to trust. Abby knew firsthand about that. She'd trusted Kevin, and look how that turned out.

"I researched him online, too." Bethany looked over her mug, exasperation in her eyes. "I'm not gullible. You don't have to worry about some guy feeding me a line to get me into bed. Or worse."

In other words, you're not like me.

"I could wait to change my name until you and Sam get married."

Abby sputtered on a mouthful of tea. Careful not to spew it all over the sofa, she emptied her mouth into the mug then wiped her face with a tissue from her robe pocket.

"Are you okay?" Bethany rushed over with the box of tissues from the end table next to her chair. "I didn't mean to make you choke."

"No problem. Nothing a few tissues can't handle. Whatever gave you that crazy idea about Sam and me?"

"K-i-s-s-i-n-g," she sang, "in the backyard."

"It's a long distance between a casual kiss and a wedding." That sounded so prissy Abby almost apologized. She sure didn't want her daughter to think that she and Sam . . .

Bethany laughed. "That wasn't a casual kiss in the snowbank. Or when we left."

"I didn't think you saw that last one."

"Good." Bethany smirked. "Better be careful. You never know who's watching." On that note, she took both mugs out to the kitchen, before returning.

"Night, Mom. Don't stay up too late. More sales tomorrow."

After Bethany gave her a quick kiss, Abby clasped her wrist. "I'm not going to marry anyone. Your father was enough for me."

"Never say never." As she skipped down the short hall, her light laughter followed.

No more marriages for her. *Once burned, twice shy.* Not that she was shy, but she sure had been burned.

She and Sam Watson would be friends. Step-siblings. That was all.

CHAPTER EIGHT

After four days of sales, Abby actually looked forward to taking inventory. She'd been right about depleting the stock. With the latest inventory from the computer attached to a clipboard, she proceeded to physically count what she had left.

She enjoyed the quiet time with her store closed. Humming along with the music softly playing in the background, she quickly finished the outer rows. A tentative knock on the door interrupted. An eager face pointed to the locked door, despite the "Closed for Inventory" sign.

Reluctantly, Abby opened the door. "The store is—"

At the same time, the woman said, "I need a gift for—"

"The store is closed," Abby said firmly. Never mind she'd lose a sale.

"Please, please, please." The vaguely familiar woman put her hands together in prayer. "I'll pay full price. I totally forgot my niece's birthday, and I saw the perfect sign for her new house. It won't take any time because I remember where it is. Uh, was, last week."

Why didn't you buy it last week?

Of course, Abby didn't say that out loud. The woman who lived in Country Club Estates had come in a few times recently. She scooted around Abby then headed for the side wall. Where Abby had just finished counting.

A minute later, she came around the corner triumphantly holding up a wood sign, "House Rules" that included Biblical references for how families should behave, one of Abby's best sellers.

"This is perfect. I know I should have bought it when I saw it. Thank you so much." She handed Abby her credit card. "I'm going to tell all my friends about you."

"But, please, tell them the store is closed until after the new year."

"Oh, I will. I promise not to tell them how kind you were to let me in while you're doing inventory. I know it's a great inconvenience."

After Abby rang up the purchase and placed the sign in a bag, she said, "Thank you for your purchase. I hope to see you again . . . after the first of the year."

The woman returned her smile and, again, gushed her thanks. "Happy New Year!"

Once she left the shop, Abby relocked the door. If she had shades, she'd pull them so nobody else would think she was open. She grumbled on the way back to the aisle where she'd left her clipboard. After marking the change for the purchase, she began again.

Another knock.

Why can't people read?

She stomped to the window next to the front door, only to discover no one there.

The knock came again.

Dang it. The back door. Must be the delivery guy. But when she opened the door, she found a smiling Sam holding a fast food bag.

"Thought you could use some sustenance during inventory. That's a pain in the butt."

"Yeah, especially when people want to come in." When Sam's smile faded, she realized what she'd said and her grumpy tone. "Not you. A persuasive customer just left. And I'm ticked off at myself for giving in."

"Did she buy something?"

"Oh, yes, so I guess I shouldn't complain. C'mon in. I'm starving."

She cleared a space on the table in the back room while Sam opened the bag and spread out a feast. Enough for two people. She was delighted he wanted to eat with her.

"You are so thoughtful." She grabbed a French fry. "I don't eat fast food often. Not that I have anything against it. I don't have time to run out."

"Where's Bethany? Isn't she helping you?"

Abby realized that though Sam had hung his jacket on the back of his chair and joined her at the table, he wasn't eating. "She's working at the Golden Fleece today and through the end of the year. Oh, did you bring something for her? Go ahead and eat it. She'll be eating much better at the restaurant."

"Chicken or burger? Your choice." When she took the chicken sandwich, Sam unwrapped his sandwich. "I haven't been there, but I've heard great things about the restaurant." He bit into his burger. "Mmm. I haven't had one of these in months."

"Really? I thought hotshot stock traders lived on fast food."

"Or takeout. Usually something we can eat at the desk. But I'm not sure about the hotshot reference."

"That's what the whole town says. Then they speculate on why you're here and not in New York City." She raised her eyebrow.

"Are you asking?" His smile reassured her that she hadn't crossed the privacy line.

"Yeah. I guess I am. I mean, who leaves the big city to retire in sleepy Far Haven, Michigan at the age of forty?"

"Thirty-eight."

"Oops. Sorry."

"No problem." He took a sip of his milkshake. "I had to make some major lifestyle changes. Dad offered me a place to stay while I, uh, worked on those changes."

Abby propped her elbow on the table. "What kind of lifestyle changes?"

"Career, diet, location."

She seized on the last word. "Are you staying around here?" *Please say yes.* Then Abby wondered why that seemed so important to her.

"I haven't decided yet."

A surprising sadness filled Abby. She mentally scoffed. *Why should I care whether he stays or goes? Typical guy. He steals a few kisses, I build up hope, then it's so long and farewell.*

"Though I'm leaning toward staying," Sam continued.

"Oh." Ashamed of her previous thoughts, Abby grimaced.

"Is that a good 'oh' or . . ." He wobbled his hand.

"Good?"

"But you're not sure. I understand." He stood and gathered the remains of their lunch.

The disappointment in his expression bothered her. What should she have done or said? Jumped up and down and screamed *Yay*?

"I'll let you get back to your inventory." He picked up his jacket.

"Sam, stay. I didn't express myself well."

He left the jacket on the chair but didn't sit. "Do you know your face is very expressive?"

"Is that good or bad?"

"Sometimes good. When I said I wasn't sure if I was staying, you had a fierce, disgusted look on your face."

"Sorry." Heat rushed into her cheeks. She looked up at him. "If you're staying—here, I mean." She pointed to the table. "Would you sit down so I don't get a crick in my neck?"

He leaned over and kissed her lightly on the lips. "Abby, you are going to drive me crazy."

Then, while her mouth hung open, he sat.

"Have you been to the Golden Fleece?" he asked.

His change of subject left her head spinning.

"No. Ever since it opened I've thought about it." She shrugged.

"What? No date ever took you there?"

She made a rude noise. "I'm sure Mother has told you. I don't date."

He leaned back in the old kitchen chair she'd appropriated from Mother's attic and stretched his legs. "Are you against dating?"

She caught the twinkle in his gray eyes. "Nope. No askers."

"Are the guys in this town stupid? A beautiful woman like you should have suitors lined up around the block."

She made another rude noise.

"What? You don't think you're beautiful?"

"Hardly. I'm a thirty-seven-year-old woman with a daughter about to go off to college. And the guys in this town are either married, old bachelors set in their ways, or divorced. Besides, I've known most of them since kindergarten."

"You don't know me." With his arms folded across his broad chest, and his long legs stretched out, he looked comfortable . . . and pleased with himself.

"No, I don't." She paused. "But I think I'd like to."

A smile curved his lips.

"After all, your dad and my mother are . . ." She let her voice trail off when Sam's smile disappeared, and his face closed up.

"I blew it again," she said. "Didn't I?"

"Yep. You really know how to put a guy in his place."

"Dang it. Here you're being so nice by bringing me lunch, and I insult you. I'm sorry."

He slouched in the old kitchen chair. "I have a question. Is it me? Or are you so out of practice that you've forgotten how to talk to a guy who's interested in you?"

She sat back, stunned. "You're interested in me?"

Using the heal of his hand, Sam thunked his forehead. "I guess my hints were too subtle. I don't usually have that problem."

"I'll bet you don't. Women probably line up around the block to get your attention."

"Maybe down the street but not around the block." He grinned.

"It's a small town."

He laughed at her dry come-back. "I'll have you know I've been hit on by no less than ten women in this small town. Some were as old as your mother, and some were even wearing wedding rings."

"Are you bragging?"

"Teasing. Of all the women I've met in this town, you're the only one who hasn't hit on me. That makes me wonder why."

She stood. "I have to get back to work. The inventory won't get done with me sitting here chit-chatting."

Leaving his chair, he blocked her way. "I am interested, Abigail Ten Eyck. And right now I want to kiss you."

His eyes darkened. She wasn't that inexperienced she didn't know what it meant. *Dang.* He really did want to kiss her.

"I'm out of practice," she admitted, not differentiating between kissing and knowing when a man wanted her to.

"Not that out of practice, if Christmas Day was any indication." Ah, he meant kissing. She wasn't sure what *she* meant.

It was going to be so hard to say what she wanted. "I think I want . . . to kiss you, too."

"Go for it."

Without putting a hand on her, he leaned in until his lips came close without touching. She closed her eyes, expecting him to complete the contact. Instead, he did nothing.

Why was he waiting?

She opened her eyes to find him watching her. *Dang.* He was waiting for her to make the move. He'd initiated their kisses on Christmas. Now he seemed determined to force her into making a decision.

Just like Kevin. He would get her all hot and bothered then withdraw.

She stepped back. She wouldn't be manipulated like that. Never again.

Without looking at him, she said, "Thank you again for lunch. It's time for you to leave."

Before he could respond, she scooted around him and out into the shop. She found her clipboard then checked where she'd left off.

"What just happened?" Sam had followed her.

"I have to finish the inventory."

He took the clipboard out of her hand. "Look at me. Please."

The tacked on "please" made her do it. She expected to see the smug look Kevin used to give her. Instead, she saw real confusion. Sam deserved an explanation, though she was loathed to do it.

"Ferret Face would do that. Tease me into wanting a kiss—or sex—then go all cold, making me feel . . ." God, she hated to admit the rest. "Making me feel foolish."

Sam put his arms around her. He tucked her head into his shoulder. "I didn't mean that. I wanted you to take the initiative. I wanted to know if you really wanted to kiss me."

While his voice rumbled in his chest, she felt the vibrations under her ear. She also heard more than the words. Sincerity, with a tinge of uncertainty. He gave her a quick hug then released her.

"Ferret Face?"

Embarrassment burned her cheeks. "I work so hard not to say that in front of Bethany. I didn't want her to get the wrong impression of her father." She scoffed. "Seems he did that all by himself. She wants to change her last name to mine in March, when she turns eighteen."

"Hmm."

She could feel his unasked question. "He doesn't visit or take her on weekends. Not since she was ten, when she started asking him questions about why he forgot her band concert or why he made excuses for not coming to get her. No phone calls, cards, or email. She said since he doesn't care about her, she wants nothing to do with him, not even his name."

Sam nodded. "I can understand her thinking." Like she tried when Bethany mentioned her plan, he sounded nonjudgmental. "I feel sorry for him. He has no idea what a wonderful girl he fathered."

"She is a wonderful girl, uh, woman. I need to remind myself that she grown up."

With his hands on her shoulders, Sam rubbed the tops with his thumbs. Tiny circles that sent big heat through her. "The credit for such a wonderful young woman goes to you. You've done a terrific job with her. I envy your closeness."

"Were you close to your mother?"

"I was a pain in the butt at Bethany's age. To both my parents." He chuckled. "I pushed limits, mouthed off, bent rules until they broke."

"What did your folks do?" She knew what she would do if Bethany ever tried any of that stuff.

"Mom pinched my ear so hard I thought I would lose it after I mouthed off once too often. Dad grounded me and took away the car keys. After he made me feel guilty for making Mom cry." His mouth quirked in a wry smile. "I didn't know I'd made her cry. That made me settled down."

"So, you were a real terror at seventeen?"

"Yep. I'm not proud of that, either. Especially when she got sick. I regretted so much then. I wanted to rewind my life and do it over." Evidence of his regrets flashed across his expression.

"We all make stupid decisions and regret them. Listen, I really do need to do the inventory." She took the clipboard he still held.

"I thought you wanted to kiss."

Knowing that she might give in to temptation, she gave him a quick kiss on the lips then bustled away.

"Oh, no. You're not getting away with that poor excuse for a kiss." He caught up with her, laughing as he took her in his arms.

"I have to finish the inventory."

"Excuses, excuses. What other topic are you going throw between us to keep from giving me a proper kiss?"

"I'm not making excuses." Though she puffed herself up in indignation, she knew he was right. Wanting to kiss him and doing it twisted her mind in confusion. Damn Kevin for feeding her insecurities. *Nobody can make you feel insecure without your consent.* Somehow Eleanor Roosevelt's quote registered more strongly than ever.

"Okay, kiddo. Fish or cut bait."

"Huh?" She snapped her head up.

"Make a decision." His breath tickled her lips.

Dang. He wasn't going to help her.

She stood on her toes and leaned forward, enough to touch his lips. Warm lips. Lips that didn't move. Lips that did nothing but be there. So unlike his Christmas kisses when they teased and coaxed. *Dang it.* She nipped his lower lip before sucking it into her mouth. He groaned but still didn't move his lips.

"Aren't you going to cooperate?" she asked.

"You're doing fine by yourself."

After snaking her arms around his neck, she scooted closer, pressing her body to his. What a wondrous feeling, one she'd missed for so long. As his body tightened, she marveled that she could do that to him. A very heady feeling.

She started out slowly, kissing the corner of his lips. Knowing he liked it, she again sucked on his lower lip. She traced his lips with her tongue before venturing to go deeper. This time he cooperated. He opened his mouth for her and let her enter and explore.

That heady feeling came again as she felt his body react. Marvelous. He tightened his arms around her then pressed his hand against her lower back. More than marvelous. His hunger seemed to match hers. She wanted to feel more of him.

Bam, bam, bam.

It took several seconds before Abby realized someone was banging on the back door. She and Sam broke away at the same time. Talk about spoiling the mood. The banging resumed.

"Hang on," she called as she raced to the door.

"About time," Bethany said as she rushed inside. "What took you so long?"

"Why are you here?" Abby asked. "And where's your key?"

"I left my key upstairs. I told you I'd help with inventory." She took off her jacket and hung it on one of the chairs at the table. "Oh, hi, Sam. I didn't know you were—"

Abby felt her daughter's eyes take in everything—her mussed hair, her shirttail pulled out of her jeans, then Sam's rumpled look and her own blush.

"Hmm. Now what were you two doing? As if I couldn't guess."

Abby's cheeks grew hotter. "None of your business, young lady. I thought you were going to spend the day with your new boyfriend. Brad? Brent?"

"Scott. I told you he and I were going to go skiing at Mount Trashmore. We did already."

"Mount Trashmore?" Sam raised his eyebrows.

"The old dump," Abby explained. "They covered it with dirt and grass and made it into a ski resort. Its real name is Lake Michigan Highlands."

"That's recycling in a big way," he said.

Bethany planted her hands on her hips. "You are playing *Grandma* by changing the subject. By the way, Scott isn't my boyfriend. We're just friends."

"Uh huh." Abby gave her a knowing smile.

"What were you two doing that made you blush, Mom, and Sam look uncomfortable?" Her stern words and expression soon morphed into a grin. "WTG, Sam."

"WTG?" he asked.

"Way to go," Abby explained. "What do you mean about that, Miss Know-It-All?"

Bethany grabbed her jacket. "I guess you have enough help with the inventory."

Sam held up his hand. "I'm sure your mother would appreciate your help. I seem to be in the way." He winked at Abby.

"I wouldn't say that," Abby said. "Bethany, please stay." That would be best. Sam was too big a distraction.

"I will see you later." Sam put on his own jacket. "Dinner tonight?"

Abby couldn't think what to say. She wanted to see him, yet she needed to finish the inventory. "I, uh, I—"

"Go to dinner with him, Mom. You need a break."

"The inventory—"

"—will be done if we get to it right away." Bethany finished her sentence then grabbed a clipboard and headed to the front of the store.

Sam pulled Abby into the back room. "I'll pick you up at seven. Does that give you enough time?"

"Yes, no. I don't know."

"We could try out the Golden Fleece. Or somewhere else?"

"Uh, well, uh." She couldn't stop sputtering. "See what you do to me?"

"Me?" He pointed to his chest . . . and grinned. She wanted to smack him.

"I'm never indecisive. I want to go to dinner with you but . . ."

He wrapped his arms loosely around her waist. "But? Are you concerned about Bethany?"

"Yes. Sort of. I haven't dated anyone lately. I'm not sure how she's going to take it."

"Considering her WTG when she thought we'd been making out, I think she's okay with us dating."

Reluctantly, she nodded.

"And you haven't dated since your divorce?"

"Yes, but not lately. I've been asked," she added quickly. "I haven't wanted to go out."

"And now you do?"

"I'm not sure." As she watched the light in his eyes dim, she took a deep breath. "Yes. I do. Dinner. I'll be ready at seven."

Abby's indecision stayed with Sam on his drive home. He could feel her warring emotions, saw them in her expressive eyes. She was shaken by their kisses and her own eagerness for them. Embarrassed when her daughter realized what they'd been doing. Scared by what she felt. The worst was her insecurity. He hated that she felt that way about herself. Punching out her ex wouldn't be good enough.

Through his dad, Sam knew about her lack of dating. He hadn't realized she hadn't in a long while. And, he assumed, she'd been celibate for just as long, if not longer. Damn that ex-husband. Damn him for taking away her confidence.

At least, Sam had gotten her to accept his offer for dinner.

"Why are you so happy?" Dad asked as he came in whistling.

"I'm taking Abby to dinner. Where's a good place in Grand Rapids? I think she'll prefer the anonymity of the city, rather than here where everyone knows her."

"Good thinking. I did the same with Flo, at first." George paused. "The Golden Fleece is nice. Good food, quiet atmosphere."

Sam shook his head. "Bethany works there. Abby might be uncomfortable."

"Right. I forgot." He named three other restaurants where he'd taken Flo.

Sam settled on one and made a reservation. He whistled as he walked down the short hall to his room. At the doorway, he stopped.

His room.

This was his dad's place. He needed to get his own place. He hadn't felt the urgency before. His former energy had taken a long time to return. Now he realized he'd become too complacent, too willing to continue the status quo.

With Flo about to put her house up for sale, she was either going to buy her own condo or move in with Dad. Whatever she did impacted Sam. He accepted, in fact, rejoiced that Dad had found someone to love, someone who loved him in return.

Mom had been the driving force in the family. She'd ordered her men around like they were foot soldiers and she their general. But she'd done it in such a loving, teasing way they'd let her. Neither had realized when her forgetfulness went beyond the everyday *senior moments*—that they were a sign of more to come. When she came out of the drugstore one day, she couldn't remember where she was or how to get home. That had scared her so much, she refused to drive again.

Sam noticed the changes when he made one of his rare trips home to Ann Arbor. When he expressed his concern, Dad admitted he'd taken her to a neurologist who confirmed their worst fears. Alzheimer's.

Watching Mom decline had been hardest on Dad. Losing the woman he'd loved for over thirty years had put him into such a depressed state that Sam feared he'd lose both his parents. Not that he could help Dad. His job—that infernal job—kept him in New York while Dad struggled by himself.

Now after four years alone, Dad had finally found another woman to love. Sam envied him. His dad had had two women, Sam none. He'd thought Nadine—

Water under the bridge. Nadine had shown her true colors when he'd gotten sick. When she left, he hadn't hurt as much as he should have. A sign he hadn't been as involved as he thought.

Abby was different. Independent, a soft center surrounded by a hard shell. That sounded like a candy. Sam stretched out on the bed and thought about those sweet kisses.

CHAPTER NINE

When Abby opened the door that evening, Sam sucked in a breath. *Holy shit*. She looked fabulous. Her hair, caught up high in back, with curls cascading from a jeweled clip. She wore gold studs in her ears. And makeup applied with a light hand. A touch of blush and very pale eyeshadow. Her lipstick, a medium pink, made her lips even more kissable.

But it was her dress that piqued his interest. An elegant black dress with crisscross straps at the top of the bodice. He wondered if the straps continued down her back. Her only jewelry, besides the earrings, was a gold necklace from which hung an aquamarine pendant. The dress hit the tops of her knees. She wore semi-sheer black tights and black strappy heels, both of which emphasized her long legs. All kinds of scenarios raced through his mind. Scenarios where he removed her dress, leaving her in black panties and thigh-high stockings. Or just the stockings and those strappy heels while her long legs wrapped around him—

Damn, he was getting hard just looking at her. *Down boy. Play the gentleman.*

"Wow. You clean up well." He grinned.

"So do you." She returned his smile.

Under his Burberry trench coat, he wore a charcoal gray suit that had been too small on him before his illness. Now it fit well. The way a thousand-dollar suit should.

"Hey, Sam." Bethany came up behind Abby. "You look great."

He gave her a nod of thanks.

"Rule #1." She ticked off on her fingers. "No kissing on the first date. Number two. If at any time you feel uncomfortable, call. I will—"

When Sam caught sight of a blush creeping across Abby's cheeks, he said, "Your rules?"

"I hate it when my words come back and bite me."

"Number three," Bethany continued.

"Enough." Abby held up her hand. "Poor Sam is still standing in the doorway."

"You didn't invite him in?" Bethany looked askance. "Would you like to come in, Sam? See, Mom, that's how it's done." She grinned.

"I will, thank you, if only to get your mother's coat."

"I have it right here." Bethany held out a red wool coat.

"Oh, not that one," Abby said. "It's too . . . too . . ."

Surprised at the color, Sam took the coat and held it for her. "It's just right."

"But—"

"You love this coat, Mom. Now get out of here, you two." Bethany wiggled her fingers.

On the way downstairs, Abby said, "This coat is too bright. I look like a stoplight."

Sam chuckled. "It suits you. And you do not look like a stoplight. You might stop traffic, though, looking as fabulous as you do."

As he held the outer door for her, she protested again. "I should go back and get my gray coat."

"No, you shouldn't." He held her arm, almost frog-marching her along the cleared sidewalk to his

SUV. "If you didn't like this coat, why did you buy it?"

She sighed and stepped up into his vehicle. "I didn't."

Since she didn't appear to be forthcoming, he closed her door and jogged around to the other side. The snow had melted last week. All that remained of winter was brown grass and mud as the ground began to thaw.

After he started the engine, he turned to face her. "You didn't buy it?"

She busied herself buckling her seatbelt. "Bethany did. Last Christmas. She thought I needed more color in my life. I was quite angry with her for wasting her hard-earned money on something so frivolous. Until I realized how hurt she was. I also found out Mother had helped her pay for it."

"But you haven't worn it, have you?"

"No." In the light of the streetlamp, he caught her look of chagrin. "She meant well."

He put the car in gear and headed toward the highway. "I don't understand why you object to the color. It's great."

"I feel—I don't know. Like I'm standing out."

"You are with that dress. But you don't want to stand out, do you? You'd rather blend into the background."

"How did you know?"

He wasn't sure how he knew. He'd never been that observant before. Too busy to give a thought to what the women he dated wore. Even Nadine. She made a point of letting him know.

"My magical ESP. The Great Watson knows all."

Pleased when she laughed at his silliness, he went on, "You are thinking this man is crazy and wondering why you ever accepted his invitation to dinner."

The trip to the restaurant went by quickly. Sam was a great entertainer. He could laugh at himself, something Abby had yet to learn. She wished she hadn't made such a big deal over the coat. It did go well with her black dress. Before they entered the restaurant, she caught a glimpse of a sophisticated woman in the window. *Who was that?* When she felt Sam's hand at her waist, and the window reflected that, she realized the sophisticated woman was her.

He made her see herself in a new way.

Still pondering that heady feeling, she let him lead her to a quiet booth. She barely heard the hostess recite the specials of the day. Only when Sam asked if she liked salmon, did she pay attention.

"Your eyes glazed over when the hostess mentioned the specials. Are you all right?"

"Sorry. Wool gathering. I don't care for salmon. Did she mention anything else?"

After Sam told her, she opened the menu. Her eyes popped when she saw the prices. "Sam," she whispered. "This place is too expensive. We should go somewhere else."

"I can afford it, you know." A hint of anger shadowed his eyes. "You don't like calling attention to yourself. How would it be if we walked out right after being seated?"

Heat filled her face. "I'm sorry. I insulted you."

"Yes, you did." His response startled her. "But I'm tough—" How quickly his eyes changed from that hint of anger to twinkling. "—I can take it. Besides you meant well."

"Oh, God." She groaned. "I seem to say all the wrong things around you." She picked up the menu, mainly to hide her face.

He gently lowed her menu then clasped her hand. "Why do I make you nervous?"

Because he looked so sincere, she decided to tell him the truth. "I was married to a man who delighted in making me uncomfortable. I didn't realize how insidious that was until after I left. I vowed never to let anyone get close enough to make me feel that way again."

Sam waved the server off with "Give us a few minutes." He continued to hold her hand. With his thumb, he rubbed along the top.

Strange, unfamiliar sensations arose from that gentle gesture.

"I don't want to make you uncomfortable. How about we look at this as two friends going out to dinner? You do go out with friends, right?"

She nodded. "Women friends."

"Would it help if you thought of me as a woman?"

She burst out laughing then quickly covered her mouth. Too late. Several people glanced over at her. Sam merely smiled then greeted the server.

"What can I bring you to drink?" She rattled off soft drinks, a number of IPA beers, and cocktails.

"Water is fine for me," she said, not knowing what she wanted.

Sam said, "Bring us a split of Pinot Grigio. Plus water for both of us."

After the server left, she said, "Thank you. I didn't want pop, and I rarely drink. Too many choices."

"I thought as much. If you don't like the wine, you can order something else." He picked up his menu. "I'm going to have the salmon special. What looks good to you?"

"Perch. I love perch." She closed the menu and set it aside.

"That surprised me. Not that you like perch, but that you made up your mind so quickly."

"I can decide." She let a small grin escape. "When I want to."

They chatted about inconsequential things through the wait for the server to order and then for the food to arrive. As they finished their meals, Sam brought up the subject of their parents.

"I'm glad Dad found your mother. She makes him laugh. I haven't seen him so energized since Mom died, and even before."

"On Christmas Day, you mentioned she had Alzheimer's."

"Yes. We both went through a difficult time. Dad more so than me. My job kept me in New York. I barely got home on weekends. Dad cared for her at home until she became violent. My sweet mother, who never swore, cussed like a trucker. When she picked up a knife and threatened him with it, he had to call the police. Worse thing he ever had to do. An ambulance took her to the hospital. Afterwards, he put her in a nursing home. She changed dramatically after that. Docile, accepting. He brought her home again. She died shortly after. I think she just gave up."

Aghast at the violence, she tried to think of what to say. "That must have been hard on you."

"More on Dad. I didn't know about her violence until later. That incident wasn't the first time. He never told me. He said he wanted me to remember her as she was. I let him shield me from the ugliness that's part of the disease. I should have been there to help him."

His anguish tore into her heart. Awful enough to know how bad off his mother was, but to have his father keep all that from him must have been worse.

Sam cleared his throat. "Enough talk about depressing things. I guess I wanted you to know how special your mother is to my dad."

"I understand. My mother has always been a scatterbrain. Many times she leaps before she thinks."

"As evidenced by the dumpster debacle."

Abby groaned. "Exactly. Bethany pointed out that she's happy, that she smiles and laughs more than we can remember. When Father was alive, she maintained a proper dignity, one befitting the wife of a well-known lawyer. At times, she was quite stuffy. She was always admonishing me to behaved properly."

"Like 'what will the neighbors think?' when we were playing on the front lawn?"

"Yes."

"I'll bet you didn't notice she was laughing."

"You're right. I didn't notice. Too busy avoiding snow down my neck." She chuckled. "By the way, I am sorry for smushing snow in your face. I couldn't resist."

"She did make us go into the backyard for privacy." His gray eyes grew dark. "For kissing and other activities."

Heat again filled her cheeks. "We only kissed."

The server took that moment to appear. Abby avoided looking at her. If she heard even half of what they said, Abby would die. Slight exaggeration. She would never come to this restaurant again. Besides, the girl didn't know her. No way would anything the server overheard get back to Far Haven.

Abby hoped.

After a moment, she said, "I wish Mother wouldn't sell the house."

Sam looked surprised. Well, that topic did come out of the blue. But, ever since Mother declared she planned to sell the house after the new year, Abby had been thinking about it. Whenever she visited, the topic became the elephant in the room. She and Mother both avoided talking about it and the argument that would, in all probability, ensue.

"She seems determined, says the house is too much for her. In a way, I see her point. It would be awful to rattle around there alone. Although I think your father often keeps her company now."

"That he does." Sam relaxed in his chair. "Why does it upset you?"

"Not your father. It's the house. I grew up there. Mother grew up there. As did her mother. It will be like losing part of my heritage. Part of me." She fiddled with her spoon. "We lived there for a while, Bethany and me, after my divorce. She talks about her fond memories. Thank goodness, she was too little to realize the tension between Father and me. He disapproved of my lifestyle."

"Why did you stay?"

"I had little money. Everything I owned fit in my Chevy Malibu. As soon as I could afford it, I leased the store from the former owner because it included the upstairs apartment. Father was not pleased."

Sam's forehead wrinkled. "Let me get this straight. Your father didn't want you living with them, yet he didn't want you to move out?"

"More he was disappointed that I didn't use my education better. Before we moved out, I finished my business associate's degree. He thought I should continue and get not just a Bachelor's but an MBA then go to work for a big firm in Grand Rapids. That wasn't what I wanted."

"And you prevailed."

"I took several business classes online. He never let me forget I didn't graduate college."

"A college degree doesn't make one successful."

He understood. How unusual. No one else did. Not her parents. Not even her friends.

"I love my shop. I love the independence. The former owner wanted to retire to Florida, so she sold the building to me. I've never regretted that."

Once again the server showed up, this time to clear dishes and ask about desserts.

"I couldn't eat another bite," she said.

"How about an after-dinner drink? Sam asked. "What would you like?"

Panicking, she froze. Not having been on a date for so long and always being the designated driver so her girlfriends could drink, she had no idea what to order. The only after-dinner drink that came to mind was sherry. That sounded like an old lady's drink. Brandy? An old man's.

"Would you like to try a Midori?" Sam must have seen her confusion.

She gave him a grateful look. "Yes, please." Then she hoped she would like whatever a Midori was.

She panicked again when Sam had decaf coffee. "Oh. I don't need a drink."

"Yes, you do. And you'll love it."

The server returned with his coffee and a glass filled with something bright green. After a sip, she said, "Ooh, this is wonderful. It reminds me of . . ." She took another sip. "Summer. A day at the beach. Is that melon?"

Sam smiled. "Yes. See, I knew you would like it. I'll bet you're a beach girl, living so close to the lake."

Remembering years past, she sighed. "I used to be. In high school, my friends and I spent a lot of time at the public beach."

"Not at the country club beach?"

"I would've had to behave there." She gave him a coy smile. "Or Father would've heard about it. Couldn't have that. 'What would the—"

"—neighbors think?',", he finished for her. "So, you were a rebellious teen?"

"Not exactly." She thought about Father, the man whose approval she had striven for. "Sometimes, I needed to blow off steam. I couldn't stay *good*—" She made air quotes. "—like Father demanded."

"Your dad didn't approve of you playing at the beach?"

"He had, uh, *expectations*. Frolicking—" She laughed. "That was what Mother called what we were doing in the snow."

"Frolicking? My dad's word was cavorting."

"Whatever. Frolicking or cavorting on the beach wasn't on Father's list of approved pastimes."

"He had a list?"

"He did. And for Mother, too. Because of his stature in the community, we had to always be on our best behavior."

"Sounds like a lot of restrictions."

"And you know what happens when a teen has too many restrictions."

"She rebels?"

"Ferret Face." She slapped her hand over her mouth. "Oh, gosh, I need to stop calling him that. I ran away and got married to someone Father forbid me to date."

"That's a little extreme."

"Oh, yeah. Turned out Father was right." She looked down at the tablecloth that she'd been worrying with her unused spoon, then glanced up, surprised to see Sam patiently waiting for her to continue. "The only good thing that came out of that disaster was Bethany. And if given the choice, I would've done it again to get her."

Sam pondered their conversation later that night. He certainly understood Abby better. She had heartache, disappointments, and joy in her life. Even if she hadn't mentioned her daughter, he had seen firsthand how much Abby rejoiced in having Bethany.

After he dropped her off, with a brief good-night kiss, he drove to the public beach. Sand covered the roadway in parts, making driving treacherous. No way did he want to go off the pavement and get stuck. He parked in front of the playground, empty swings flapping intermittently with gusts of wind. Giant iceballs stood out near the shore, while waves splashed high on the ice-covered channel markers.

Since coming to west Michigan, he'd found how easy it was to think while watching the waves. In the fall, they'd been gentle at times, stormy and wild at others. A lot like his life. The wild and crazy turbulence of the marketplace had energized him, the adrenaline of timing the market had made him a stellar performer. It also contributed to the decline of his health. He enjoyed the quiet of a calm lake. Yet, he missed the excitement.

After turning off the engine, he debated walking along the shore. Because of their date, he hadn't worn a heavy coat. When he stepped out of the SUV, the icy wind cut through his overcoat and suit jacket. What was he thinking? He retreated to the warmth of the car's interior.

Now that his body was healing, his mind needed . . . something. Some excitement in his life. Abby. She definitely excited him. Confused him. Challenged him.

His work in Dad's garage kept his hands busy. Concentrating on delicate scrollwork for each doll's house gave his restless mind a respite. Courting—such a charming word—Abby made him feel alive again.

Moonlight glinted on the ice-covered lake. After resting his head back, he gave long thought to something that had niggled in his mind since Christmas. He needed to go home to his computer and make plans.

Abby finished inventory on New Year's Eve. She'd found a few discrepancies between what her computer inventory reported and the physical one. She chalked up the losses to mistakes or theft. She'd have to keep a closer eye on the trinkets. Or move the displays closer to the register.

Sam walked in while she struggled with a display. "Let me help you."

When they got it in place, he asked, "Why didn't you call me? I would've been over sooner."

She shrugged.

He arched his eyebrow. "Little Miss Independent?"

"You know me well." She chuckled. "What brings you out on a blustery winter day?"

"To find out what you're doing tonight."

"Same old, same old. Watch a movie, eat popcorn, and check out the ball dropping in New

York City then go to bed. What about you? Oh. I'll bet you stood in Times Square when you lived there. Was it as exciting as it looks?"

"You mean wall-to-wall people stepping on each other's feet, getting elbowed right and left, pickpockets' hands in my back pocket or—" He made a face. "—elsewhere. Nah. Never been there."

With a laugh, she parked on the stool behind the counter. "I'll bet you had an apartment on the ninety-something floor where you could look down on all those people and the festivities."

"Twentieth floor." He got a faraway look before adding, "Oddly, last year's celebration was exactly like yours, minus the popcorn."

"No popcorn? That's blasphemous. You can't watch a movie without popcorn."

"You can if you'll spend all night afterward in the john."

"Really? Oh. You must be allergic to the butter. I noticed at dinner you seem to be careful about what you eat."

He sighed. "Not lactose intolerant. Ulcers. Back to my original question. What—"

"Ulcers? Tell me about that."

"I don't talk about it." His tone had turned gruff, before he cleared this throat. "It's personal."

"I told you personal stuff on our date."

"I thought it wasn't a date, just dinner with a friend." A twinkle appeared in his eyes. He looked so approachable with those twinkles and the dimple in his cheek when he grinned.

"You're right. Not a date. Quit changing the subject." She grabbed his hand and tugged him nearer. "Would you be more at ease if you sat? I can get—"

He stopped her from jumping off the stool. "I don't need to sit. Let's see how to put this."

"You're stalling. Just hit me with it. No sugar coating."

"Okay. I let the stress of my job eat away at my guts. Hospital. Diet lectures. Hospital. More lectures. Therapy. Rinse and repeat until I got the message. Is that enough?"

"Succinct. You don't eat popcorn with movies. Got it." She got it, all right. The man had a hard head, didn't listen to doctors, and finally did. "Surgery?"

He nodded. "Is it okay if we go back to my original reason for coming here?" He stared at her while twisting his mouth. When she nodded, he said, "Would you like company for that movie and watching the ball drop at midnight?"

"Oh. You want to spend New Year's Eve with me?"

He knocked on her forehead. "Duh. You are so quick on the uptake. Yes, I would like to spend New Year's Eve with you."

"Of-Of course. It won't be a very exciting evening for you."

"It's what I'd like to do. I've had *exciting* evenings, and an evening of watching movies with you, on your couch, will be vastly better."

Dressed in jeans and a flannel shirt, Sam rang Abby's doorbell. He thanked the stars that her door faced east, avoiding the bitter wind raging across Lake Michigan. Enough whipped around the corner to cut through his open jacket. This winter made him grateful for the brilliant designers at Carhartt.

After being buzzed in, he took the stairs two at a time. He wasn't excited or anything, he grinned. He'd spent New Year's Eve at high-end restaurants and at lavish parties, yet he looked forward to spending the evening with Abby more than any other event.

When he approached the landing, she opened the door. He was pleased to see she'd dressed like him, casual and comfortable. Except she wore thick wool socks. Christmas socks, red with white snowflakes and reindeer. He removed his boots, leaving them on the mat beside the door.

"I made snack-y things that we can graze on during the movie. I looked up what you should and shouldn't eat. I hope that's okay. And if you can't eat something or don't like it, that's okay. Don't feel—"

He pulled her into his arms and kissed her. Long, gentle then harder as she wrapped her arms around his neck and kissed him back.

"Hey, aren't you guys supposed to wait until midnight?" Bethany stood about ten feet away.

By golly, he hadn't even seen her come in. Or was she there when he entered? Focused on Abby, he hadn't paid attention.

"That's one way to shut Mom up." With a wink, she edged past them to open the closet door. "Can I take your jacket, Sam?"

As he took off his jacket, he looked more closely at Bethany. She wore a black, strapless sequined top, wide-legged black slacks, and strappy sandals.

"You look lovely," he said. "Do I take it you aren't watching movies with us?"

She laughed. "You old folks party your way, and I'll party mine." She pulled the red coat out of the closet and slipped it on. "Have fun, you two." She wiggled her fingers.

Right on time, the doorbell rang. She pressed the intercom. "Be right down, Tom."

When the door slammed behind her, Sam grinned. "Alone at last. Shall we pick up where we left off?"

Abby backed up. "Maybe later. Come and load up a plate."

"I'd rather kiss," he groused but followed her out to the kitchen. "But if it makes you happy—" He stopped and looked at the spread. "Wow. Who else is coming?"

He found her blush endearing.

"Just us. You didn't tell me what kind of movies you like. I hope you don't mind I pulled out a few of my favorite DVDs. My feelings won't be hurt if you don't like any. We can run down to the drugstore and hit Red Box if—"

Once again, he took her into his arms. "Are you that nervous?" He pulled her closer. "Do I have to kiss you again to keep you from rambling?"

"Sorry. I just—oh, kiss me and then let's eat."

"How can I resist such an invitation?" He dipped her over his arm and laid one on her.

When he righted her, she looked dazed and thoroughly kissed. "Taking lessons from your dad?" Reminding him of Christmas day under the mistletoe.

"Who better?" Following her lead, he filled a plate with all kinds of goodies then carried it to the living room where he set it on the coffee table. "Hmm. *Mission Impossible, Star Trek IV: The Voyage Home*—one of my favorites—*African Queen*? I haven't seen that one in years." He set the others down and kept the last. "I'm a sucker for Bogie and Hepburn."

He sat on the couch and patted the spot next to him. "Come, sit."

She took care of the DVD first then settled next to him, put her feet up on the coffee table, slouched, and set her plate on her abdomen. "Ready?" She aimed the remote at the TV.

Sam picked up his plate and imitated her position. "Ready."

Sam was so easy to be with. He made her feel . . . safe? secure? comfortable? Except when he kissed her. Then she felt edgy, thrilled, like fireworks going off inside her. Lordy, she could get used to that.

The movie ran in the background as she contemplated how the evening would end. Torn by anticipation and common sense, she missed a good part of the movie. She clutched Sam's hand as the Queen went over the rapids, then shuddered when Charlie came out of the water with leeches. Sam put his arm around her shoulder and brought her closer. She buried her head in his shoulder so she couldn't see Charlie and Rosie peel them off.

When the Queen blew up the German gunship and Rose and Charlie were treading water, Abby sighed. "I love this movie."

"I've never seen it with such a lovely companion." He leaned over and lightly kissed her lips.

Thrilled, excited beyond her imagination, she wanted more. Desperately wanted more. She scooted closer and clung to him as tightly as those leeches. She shivered at the image.

Abruptly, he stood nearly dumping her off the couch. "What can I bring you from the kitchen?"

His sudden movements discombobulated her. "Wh-What?"

"Put in another video," he called.

"Hey, what happened?" She followed him to the kitchen.

"Did I see a *Star Trek* movie on the coffee table?"

Turning him away from the snacks, she said, "Tell me what happened. One minute we're kissing, the next you drop me on the floor."

"I didn't drop you—" He stopped himself. "You're right. I wanted to go further. Much further. But, you're not ready, are you?"

She gave that some thought, knowing full well what he meant by going further. "I could be."

His smoldering look made her shiver. "Let me know when you are." He chose several hors d'oeuvres. "You don't have that *Star Wars* movie, the spin-off? Or what about a James Bond flick? I haven't seen a good action-adventure in a long time."

"You sound like a kid at a Saturday matinee."

"I haven't enjoyed watching movies like this since . . ." He wrinkled his brow. "Since I was a kid. Dad would put in a VCR tape, and Mom made popcorn. We'd watch Disney movies and action adventures or westerns. Dad loved John Wayne. He'd tease Mom about romantic comedies, but he enjoyed them as much as she did."

His enthusiasm was contagious. She talked about overnights with her friends and all the scary movies they watched without their parents' knowledge. After filling their plates, they gathered up the remains of the food, leaving out non-perishables. He filled his glass with ice water and replenished her ginger ale.

When they returned to the living room, she needed no encouragement to sit close to Sam. His arm around her shoulders seemed natural. At the beginning theme, she closed her eyes.

* **

Sam's arm was numb. He dared not move for fear of waking Abby. Her earlier nervousness was gone. She must be comfortable with him. Part of him rejoiced that she'd gotten past her tension around him. Another part of him wanted her to be more aware of him as a man. A Bond girl wouldn't fall asleep *before* making love. Afterwards, maybe.

As the ending credits scrolled up the screen, she lifted her head.

"I fell asleep." She yawned.

"Yep."

"When?"

"He was bungee-jumping over the dam."

"No. That was at the beginning." She struggled to right herself.

He held her against his chest. "That's right. It's a wonder I heard any dialogue with you snoring up a storm."

"I did not snore. Did I?" When she managed to sit upright, she caught him laughing. "Oh, you." She batted his arm. "I'm sorry. Some hostess I am."

Using the remote, Sam changed from the DVD to a live shot of Times Square. The countdown had begun. "We're just in time. Thirty seconds. Twenty-nine . . ."

At five, he looked deep into her eyes. "Happy New Year, Abby."

"Happy New Year, Sam." Without waiting for him, she launched into a kiss that knocked his socks off.

She was aware of him as a man, now. She crawled onto his lap and straddled him. Holy shit, she had her hands under his T-shirt.

"You have on too many clothes," she muttered against his mouth.

"So do you." He shrugged off his flannel shirt, which was much too warm, then helped her remove hers.

He tunneled under her T-shirt, yanked it off, and found the hooks for her bra. With a quick flick, the bra released, freeing her breasts. Within seconds, nothing separated their flesh. Panting like all the air had gone out of the room, he rested his forehead on hers.

"Should we take this into your bedroom? Before Bethany comes in."

"Bethany." Snatching her T-shirt off the couch, she held it in front of her. "Oh, my God, what am I doing?" She scrambled off his lap, nearly falling as she tried to stand. "Necking like a teenager."

With her back to him, she pulled on her shirt. When she turned back, her eyes widened. "For goodness sake, put some clothes on before she gets home."

Reluctantly, he put his shirt on. Without getting up, he held out her bra. "Missing something?"

Her eyes widened. She snatched it out of his hand and tried to stuff it into her jeans' pocket as she walked around the coffee table. "Why are you still sitting there? Get up."

"I'd rather watch you pace." He scrubbed his hand across the top of his head. "I blew it, didn't I? Mentioning Bethany."

What a dummy.

"If she had walked in . . ." Abby covered her face. "I can't believe we were . . . naked."

"Half-naked," he pointed out.

She stopped pacing and whirled around. "Do you think this is a joke?"

Slowly, he got to his feet then ambled to her. Keeping his hands at his side—heaven only knew what she'd do if he reached for her—he said, "No joke. Unless it's on me. Abby, I enjoyed kissing you. I liked your hands on me. You let yourself go, and— if I'm not mistaken—you enjoyed what we were doing. I assumed you were ready for more. Tell me I'm wrong."

Her shoulders slumped. "I can't tell you that," she said in a small voice. "I got carried away. I shouldn't have."

"Why?"

"Why? For God's sake, I'm a mother. I don't get naked with a man in my living room." She whirled away then returned. "It's time for you to go home."

"No. I'm not going home. At least, not right now. We need to talk."

"Talk? Hah. I know what you want. You want me naked, in bed. And don't say you don't."

"Huh? I almost followed that. Of course, I want you naked. Naked in bed is even better. But I've never forced a woman to do something she didn't want to do." He rubbed the tops of her shoulders. "You gave me every indication you wanted me naked. And in bed. Did I misread your signals?"

He was sure he hadn't. But, he'd been wrong before. She refused to look at him. Her silence lasted so long he shifted his sock-clad feet. He was about to let her go, when she mumbled.

"Beg your pardon? I didn't hear that." He was pretty sure he'd heard her. And her answer pleased him immensely.

She cleared her throat. "You didn't misread me. I, uh, wanted more. I, um, overreacted." She finally lifted her head. Her clear blue eyes shimmered. "I'm sorry, Sam. Please don't hate me."

"Hey, no crying on New Year's Day." With his thumb, he wiped an errant tear. "And, for the record, I don't hate you. I'm glad we got things straight. We want each other. Naked. In bed."

A rosy blush tinged her cheeks. "Must you keep repeating that?"

"Abby, I'm trying to go slow. I understand it's been a long time for you. Just when I think I've gotten your signals straight, you throw me a curve ball, and I feel like I'm back to square one."

She gave him a mutinous look. "I told you I come with baggage."

"I understand that. I'm willing to keep going slow."

"Why?" She twisted her hands. "Why do you bother with me?"

"Because I think you're worth it. Now, go in the bathroom and wipe your eyes. Don't want Bethany to come home and find you in tears. That girl will come after me with—with the shovel at the bottom of the stairs."

Finally, Abby smiled. "She would."

While she was gone, he cleaned up the kitchen. She did a lot of work on his behalf. The foods were perfect. Nobody had ever gone to that much trouble for him since before Mom's Alzheimer's kicked in. Dad had done his best, but nothing like this. Abby cared for him. That kept him from giving up on her.

"Fool," she whispered to her reflection in the bathroom mirror. "You acted like a shocked virgin, instead of a thirty-seven-year-old mother."

She held a cold washcloth to her eyes. "Buck up, girl. Go out and tell that man you want him. Naked. In your bed. Tonight."

Her reflection stared back at her. "What kind of a mother am I? I can't have a man in my bed when Bethany comes home."

She would understand.
But what kind of an example would I be?
A light rap startled her.

"Are you okay?" Sam asked through the door.
Not really. "I'll be right out."

"Take your time." His footsteps faded until he found the creaky board in the hall.

She took a deep breath and walked out of the bathroom. He wasn't standing in the hall, waiting for her. She found him in the kitchen.

"Oh, my. You didn't need to clean up."

He'd put away all the snacks, wiped down the counter, and put the dishes in the dishwasher.

"Least I could do." He straightened the towel hung over the oven door handle. "Did I blow it with you?"

When he didn't turn around, she came up behind him, wrapped her arms around his waist, and leaned her head against his back. "I'm the one who blew it. You've been nothing but a gentleman since we met. No one has ever been this patient with me. You can't imagine how good you make me feel."

He crossed his hands in front and covered her hands.

"Don't give up on me, Sam. Please?"

Giving her hands a squeeze, he turned around. "Never. I promise. Nobody's giving up on anyone."

She gave him a tiny smile. "Can I give you another New Year's kiss? Before you leave?"

"I was hoping you would. Turning me out into the dark of night, in a raging snowstorm without a kiss would be cruel and unusual punishment."

"A raging snowstorm?"

"There could be."

She slid her hands up to cup his cheeks. Holding his face still, she kissed him. "Happy New Year, Sam."

He returned her light kiss. "Happy New Year, Abby."

CHAPTER TEN

The next morning Mother called. "Are you coming over to take the tree down?"

They'd talked about it several times the previous week. "Mother, it's not even seven o'clock."

"And Happy New Year to you, too, sweetie. Did you and Sam have a good time last night?"

Did she? A small smile crept out. "Yes, Mother. We had a good time. How about you and George?"

A giggle came out of the phone. "Oh, we did." Another giggle. Then she became serious. "Remember what I said. I want to sort the ornaments as you take them down. The decorations, too."

"Sort?" Abby's muzzy head short circuited. "What do you want to sort?"

"The ornaments and decorations." Mother sounded aggravated. "I mentioned this when we decorated after Thanksgiving. We'll sort everything into what I want to keep. You and Bethany will do the same."

That sorting. Abby remembered and dreaded what was to come.

"We'll have dinner afterward. You're bringing Mac and Cheese, right?"

"Yes, ma'am. And Bethany made a cranberry salad. Is George coming?"

Actually, she wanted to know if Sam would be there. He hadn't said anything last night, rather this morning when he left.

"Of course. Sam, too. See you when you get here. I told Sam we were eating at two."

Two? Abby doubted they'd get done sorting and putting away the decorations by then. Mother's indecision would drag this project out all day, probably all week. After hanging up, Abby groaned and threw her arm across her eyes. A weak light came through her bedroom curtains. The streetlight on the corner. Too early for the sun. Too early for her.

"Morning, Mom." Bethany staggered into the bathroom. When she came out, she climbed into bed with Abby.

"You haven't done this since you were little." She wrapped her arm around her daughter.

"More like last year." Bethany scooted down under the covers. "Did you have a good time with Sam last night?"

"I did. We watched *The African Queen* and *Golden Eye*." She didn't admit to sleeping through the last movie.

"Mo-ther. Why didn't you watch something sexy? You know, to get in the mood."

"Beth-a-ny," she drew out her name. "It's not like that."

"Oh, right. You old fogeys don't like sexy movies? From that kiss Sam planted on you when he came in last night, I figured he'd stay the night."

Abby sat up. "Bethany."

"Oh, come on, Mom. He's hot. You haven't had sex since I was a baby."

"What?" Outrage warred with surprise. "How do you know I haven't had sex since—forget that. It's none of your business."

"Chill, Mom. I was teasing." She waited until Abby settled back in bed. "It would be okay with me if he did stay. I like him. He's like George with

Grandma. Sam makes you happy. Around him, you smile more than you normally do."

For several moments, Abby pondered her daughter's observation. "I am happy with him."

"I know my father did a number on you. And I'm glad you left him. Sam's a good man. Don't push him away, like you always do."

"What? I don't—"

Bethany turned on her side to face her. "You do. Those guys you dated when I was younger? You pushed them away. I didn't think you'd ever find anyone. I want you to be happy, Mom. I'm going to college across the state in the fall, and I don't want you to be lonely."

Abby pulled her close. "Oh, sweetie. Don't worry about me. I'll be fine."

She would be. Loneliness didn't factor in her consideration of Sam. They had something together. Something she never felt with Fer—Kevin.

"What time did you get in last night. I mean, this morning? Did you have a good time?"

"I think it was about two, two-thirty. We had a great time. Scott is so funny. The party was going downhill after midnight, so we ended up at Denny's and talked."

"Scott? I thought you went out with Tom."

"Him?" She made a rude noise. "He brought some whiskey and spiked the punch. I was so mad at him. Then, he was all over me."

"Sweetie?"

"I kneed him and left with Scott. His girlfriend ditched him for a college guy, somebody's brother. Scott's really sweet."

"I'm glad you got home safely. I didn't know Tom drank." She bet his mother didn't know, either.

"Mom, I know what you're thinking. Do not call his mother. I mean it. If she's half as observant as you, she'll smell alcohol all over him. Besides, he's eighteen. He's an adult."

"Technically, yes. But still too young to drink legally."

"Mom." Bethany's warning voice surprised Abby. "Do not call—"

"All right. I won't. But if his mother should bring it up . . ."

"Mom." Sharper this time.

"I won't call."

Abby smoothed her daughter's hair away from her face, the way she did when Bethany was little. Her precious daughter had grown up too quickly. Apparently, her street-smart daughter knew how to handle herself.

She and Tom's mother weren't close friends. They saw each other occasionally, usually at the store. Abby would find a way to bring up the subject of drinking. At least, there hadn't been drugs. The more she thought about it, she wondered . . .

"Were there drugs at the party?"

Bethany didn't say anything for a few moments. "I didn't see any. I heard some talk, but my friends know better than to bring up drugs in front of me."

They lazed away another hour, chatting about Bethany's friends and their plans for after graduation.

"Scott wants to be a doctor. He hopes he'll get into U of M's medical school."

"Good for him. Does he know you're going to Michigan?"

"That's not why he's going there. I'll be finished by the time he comes. He's had it all planned out for two years. He wants to go Hope for undergraduate school, University of Michigan's medical school, residency at Johns Hopkins, and a fellowship at Cleveland Clinic or Mayo." She sounded more enthusiastic for Scott than Abby had ever heard about herself.

"You two did have a long talk last night. He's got a long road ahead of him. I'm impressed."

"I'm he'll make it, Mom. He's so excited, even though he knows he'll have a lot of student loans. He's a year younger than me, yet he's more mature than some older guys, like Tom. I wished I hadn't gone out with him. What a loser."

Though she refrained from saying so, Abby was proud of her daughter for recognizing a loser when she saw him. She wished she'd had Bethany's common sense when she was that age. But then, she wouldn't have married Kevin and wouldn't have had Bethany.

"I suppose we should get up. We have to help Grandma take down the tree, and she's having dinner at two."

Bethany bounded out of bed, looking more cheerful than Abby felt. "George and Sam will be there, right?"

"Right."

"I'm so glad they're going to be part of our family."

On January third, Mother announced she'd sold the house.

Abby dropped her phone. It squirted out of her hand and slid under the counter in the store. She crawled on the floor trying to grab it while Mother kept talking. Abby could hear her voice, but what she was saying was a mystery.

Finally, she found the phone, brushed off a couple of the dustbunnies who'd escaped her vigorous cleaning the day before, and brought the phone to her ear.

"So, we have to take everything we want."

"Say again, Mother. I missed the last part."

"Abigail, listen up. I have a buyer. He wants the house as is, furniture and all. We just need to take what we want. I'm going to need your help."

"When did you put the house on the market? I thought you were going to wait until after the new year."

"This *is* the new year, dear. I didn't need to put it on the market. The buyer heard, by word of mouth, that I wanted to sell."

"Is it someone we know? Someone from here in Far Haven?" Abby couldn't control the anxiety in her voice. She hitched her hip on the stool behind the counter.

"I don't know."

"What do you mean you don't know? What's his name?"

"I don't know," Mother said with exasperation. "He wants to remain anonymous. He's working through a lawyer and, of course, Maureen Donovan. It's all on the up-and-up. Maurccn had him checked out. You know how thorough she is. She wouldn't waste time on someone who couldn't afford this house. You can't imagine what a relief it is not to have people tramping through the house, looking in cupboards and closets."

"I can't imagine anyone buying a house unseen." Abby began to freak out again. "Has he looked through the house already?"

"Yes. Maureen came over when I was at the Senior Center yesterday. Before you get all bent out of shape, I gave her permission. She suggested I have Pieter Bogardus look over the contract. Now, I won't keep you. I heard the bell ring, so I know you have a customer. I just wanted to let you know the good news."

Mother disconnected. Stunned by the *good* news, Abby hadn't heard the bell. When she looked up, Sam Watson strolled toward her.

"No customers?"

She shook her head.

"What's wrong? You look like you lost your best friend. I know that's a cliché, but it fits." He reached across the counter, tipped up her chin with his knuckle, and kissed her on the lips.

"Mother sold the house." She let her shoulders slump. "I don't know how she did it. She told me she wasn't going to put it on the market until the first of the year, which she reminded me it is. Some anonymous guy wants everything. All that antique furniture, my family heritage."

She wanted to put her head on the counter and cry.

"Hey. Maybe it will all work out." He rounded the counter and took her in his arms. "Please don't cry. I don't do well with crying females." His soft laughter made her smile. "That's better. So, tell me all about the sale."

She told him as much as she knew, which wasn't much, just what her mother had conveyed. "I'm going to talk to Maureen. She's the real estate agent who's handling everything. I know she'll make sure Mother gets a good deal. They've been friends for years. I have to find out who's buying the house. I don't understand how someone heard about Mother wanting to sell. We never told anyone."

"Are you sure? Your mother talks to Dad about it all the time. How happy she'll be when she *unloads*—her word—*that monstrosity*—again, her word. I imagine everyone at the Senior Center knows."

Abby grimaced. "And her bridge group. Those ladies talk about everything. You're right. Anyone could have heard, even someone from out of town. Maybe a relative of someone here in Far Haven. I just wish he didn't want to remain anonymous. That is very strange."

"Oh, I don't know. Happens all the time in metropolitan areas. Now what happened to that tiny smile I saw a few minutes ago?"

Abby forced her mouth to curve up. A real effort. "Mother wants Bethany and me to go through the house and take anything we want. I don't have room for the boxes of ornaments and Christmas decorations I took on New Year's Day. And I know Mother will need help with her things."

"I can help. Doesn't Bethany know a couple of boys who are glad to earn some money?" He rubbed her shoulder. "It will all work out."

"I wish I had your confidence. I'm going to have to close the store for a few days. Maybe even a week." She propped her elbow on the counter and rested her forehead in her palm. "I can't even think about this."

She hopped off the stool and strode into the back room. Boxes delivered earlier sat on the floor, stacked there by the regular driver. Thank goodness, he was back. She knelt on the floor and, using a box cutter, opened the first box. She pulled out bubble wrap that cushioned the contents. Sam came up behind her and lifted her off the floor.

"I'll hand you the—whatever these are—and you sort on the table." He took her place kneeling. "Deal?"

Standing behind him, she wrapped her arms around his neck. "You are too good to me. What would I do without you?" She kissed him behind his ear.

"I hope you never find out." He twisted his head around and kissed her. "Let's get to work."

With Sam's help, she verified the invoice, carried the items out into the shop, and placed them on display. They did the same with the remaining boxes. With only a couple of customers to interrupt, they finished in no time.

"That's what happens when we work together." Sam circled her waist.

She nodded, happy to be done. "I can't deny it."

"See how relaxed you are. This is how you should be all the time."

"Whoa." She backed out of his arms. "What are you saying?"

"I hate to see you all stressed out."

"I'm not stress—"

"Not right now, but you're tightening up. It's okay, babe."

"What do you mean it's okay? What are you trying to do?"

"Keep you from making my mistakes. I don't want you, or anyone, to go through what I did."

His earnestness kept her from jumping down his throat. *He means well*, she told herself. *Remember that.*

"I said the wrong thing, didn't I?" He looked so serious . . . and nervous. "I didn't mean to upset you. I'm afraid for you, Abby. Afraid you'll work yourself into an early grave."

"Oh, Sam." She looped her arms around his neck. "I know you mean well. Is that why you drop in so often? To keep me from working too much?"

He shrugged. "Maybe. Or maybe I come by because I want to see you. And kiss you."

"How could I stay mad at you when you grin like that?" She laughed when his grin turned silly. "Don't you have your own work?"

"The great thing about being self-employed is setting my own hours. Maybe you could help me." He pointed to her computer. "I like your website. Bethany said you did it yourself. How do you feel about giving me some pointers?"

"Of course. Show me what ya got." Giving him a big grin, she pushed him onto her stool. "Photos are good. You need to show what you can do and how customers can personalize what they want."

"Maybe we can work on that after I help you sort out the things you want from your mother's."

As soon as she closed the store for the day, she and Sam headed over to Mother's. George opened the door. When he saw them, he rolled his eyes. "Flo is in a tizzy. She keeps going from one room to the next, never deciding anything. I've been here since noon, and she hasn't chosen one thing to keep."

"George? Who's at the door?" Mother's voice came from the kitchen. "Send them away. We have too much to do."

Abby scooted around George. "It's Sam and me, Mother. We came to help."

In the kitchen, Mother had emptied all the cupboards, the contents stacked on every surface. Abby groaned. How would they pack up with no place to put boxes?

"I'm so glad you're here, Abigail. George is no help."

139

Abby glanced over her shoulder at Sam's dad. Poor man. He looked like he'd been through the wringer. She steered her mother to the kitchen table. After stacking several pans that had been on a chair, she made Mother sit. "We need a plan."

"I'll say," George muttered. "I'm ordering take-out from the café. Sam, will you run out and pick it up?"

"Sure thing." Sam steered George into the dining room, where they talked so softly Abby couldn't hear.

Meanwhile, she opened drawers until she found a large notebook. "Mother, we're going to start in the living room. You tell me what you want to take to your new place. By the way, do you have a new place?"

Mother wrung her hands. "Not exactly."

"What does that mean?"

"I'm not sure if I'm going to buy that house I love on the bluffs or move in with George."

Oh, boy. It was on the tip of Abby's tongue to berate her mother. *What was she thinking? You don't sell before you know where you're going.*

Instead of bringing that up, Abby took a deep breath and blew it out. "No problem. We can put your belongings in storage until you decide."

"Oh, I don't know about storage. You know how those places are. Our antiques will be ruined."

Heaven help me. "I'll make sure we get one that's climate controlled. The important thing right now is deciding what you want to keep." Abby guided her mother into the living room.

Despite her mother's dithering—and telling convoluted stories about the history of each item— Abby managed to get her to decide on five pieces of furniture she wanted to keep. When George came in to say Sam had gone after the food, Mother was in tears.

"I didn't know it would be this hard."

When George opened his arms, she flew into them. "There, there," he murmured, along with other soothing sounds. "I know it's hard. Remember, I had to do this when I left the house where Sam grew up."

"But I've lived here so long."

"Yes. A lot longer than I did in that house in Ann Arbor." George rubbed her back. "I guess us guys aren't as sentimental as you." When Mother started to protest, he went on quickly, "That's what we love about you women. Sentimentality. You invest so much of yourself into your home."

Although Abby thought he was a bit patronizing, Mother smiled in relief.

"You understand? Oh, Georgie, you really do understand."

He smiled then kissed her cheek. "We all understand. Now, before Sam gets back, let's take a look at what you want to take."

"Oh, we're going to put my things in storage until I have my own place."

George glanced at Abby, who shrugged. Mother had made a couple of decisions without telling her. Or him.

With his encouragement, Mother made quick work of the living room. Abby followed behind them, writing like crazy. They went into the sitting room, used by the women of the family for years to write correspondence, make lists, and write down their recipes. Mother's houseplants liked that room since it got a lot of sun. Would she take those with her or leave them for the new owner, who would probably over- or under-water them and kill them off.

Mother pointed to the secretary, an ornate cherry bookcase with a drop-down lid that served as a writing surface. The beveled glass doors covered the upper shelves where a jumble of knickknacks crowded inside. Underneath, two large drawers contained linen tablecloths that didn't fit in the buffet in the dining room.

"My mother used this desk." Mother sighed as she ran her fingers over the glass frame. "She wrote letters to her cousins and friends who'd moved away. How can I part with this?"

"It's eight feet tall, Flo." George rubbed her shoulder. "I don't know of any condos with ten foot ceilings that could accommodate this."

"You mean I should leave it?" Her voice rose in distress.

"Where would you put it?" George, the voice of reason.

"I suppose you're right." She wiped a tear that ran down from the corner of her eye.

The front door opened, and Sam called out, "Dinner's here."

"Thank goodness." Mother scurried out to the dining room, while Sam and Abby gave each other commiserating looks.

They sat at the dining room table since the kitchen table held pots and pans. During a fine meal of broasted chicken, dressing, mashed potatoes and gray, plus a few different salads, Sam asked about progress.

Before Abby could speak, George said, "Remember how hard it was for me to leave our home?"

Sam smiled. "You wanted to take everything."

"But you talked me into taking only what would fit into the condo. Glad I listened to you, son."

Abby watched as his point sunk home with Mother. Usually, she was oblivious to hints. But not with George. He was having a good effect on her.

"Here's an idea," George went on. "How about I draw up floor plans for that house you like? Then it would be easier to decide what will fit."

"Oh, George, you are so clever." Mother leaned over to give him a kiss, and almost fell off her chair. "That is a marvelous idea. Do you need that special paper with tiny squares? Oh, what is it called?"

"Graph paper?" he said with more patience than Abby had.

"I think Father had some in his office." She jumped up. "I'll check."

Sam followed her.

"Your father is a godsend," Abby whispered. "If I'd suggested that, she would have made all kinds of excuses."

She entered her father's sanctuary and stood to the side of the doorway. "I wasn't allowed in here for years. Even then, I wasn't allowed to touch anything unless he specifically asked for it or gave me permission."

Shaking off the sensation that she was violating a sacred place, she marched to the desk and opened a drawer. Sure enough, she found a pad of graph paper. When she turned, she realized Sam had been watching her.

"Is this going to be as hard on you as it is on Flo?"

"For some items. Not in this room, though. After he died, I purposely came in and opened every drawer, looked in all the corners, on all the shelves. And I touched everything. Sounds petty, doesn't it?"

"No. I understand."

That, she realized, was why she lo—liked Sam.
He really did understand her.

And so it went. George drew up room plans,
and Mother made decisions. Abby and Sam
returned to their businesses but came over every
night to help. Two weeks later, Abby tackled the
attic after church. Mother took one look at the
jumbled mess and told Abby to do whatever she
wanted with the family's castoffs. Good news. Abby
could deal with the contents of a myriad of boxes
without her mother's dithering or sharing
memories, and the work would go faster.

From the handwriting on labels, many family
members had had a hand in what was stored. She
found a bookcase that would work for Bethany's
dorm plus a stuffed chair that had seen better days,
but her daughter wanted that, too. Abby worked up
a sweat shoving furniture aside, looking behind and
under or inside. Some of the boxes weren't too
sturdy, so she carefully pulled them across the attic
floor.

Sam had driven over to Detroit to deliver a
special order. She'd photographed the lovely
Victorian doll's house for his website. He'd told her
to wait until he returned so he could help with the
attic. Too anxious to get this over with, she went
ahead on her own.

While she dragged one box across the floor, the
side split. Papers and notebooks spilled out.

"Crap." She ran down to the second floor where
she'd dropped several boxes she would need to pack
up her old bedroom.

As she transferred the spilled papers into a
sturdier box, she realized that box was the one
Mother had gone ballistic over. The one she made

Abby promise to destroy without reading the contents.

"Curiosity killed the cat," Grandma Ten Eyck always said, followed by, "satisfaction brought it back."

No. She would not read her mother's personal letters and . . .

In order to get everything into the new box, Abby stacked the letters, trying very hard not to read the cramped writing. Definitely not her mother's rounded cursive. If she had to guess, she'd say it was a man's hand. Words jumped out despite her caution. She congratulated herself on her self-control. Until one word made her stop.

Baby.

Abby gasped. She turned the paper over. The signature was a heart.

She gathered the surrounding papers and took them over to the stuffed chair. And read.

Her mother had had a child by a man who wasn't her husband. If she read the letter correctly, Mother had tried to contact him. He hadn't received her letter for over a year.

Abby read his anguish that Mother had been alone. He understood why she married a persistent suitor. How sad, Abby thought. If the one-sided correspondence was any indication, Mother and the man had truly loved each other. She continued to read previous letters, then journals, a girl's confession to her diary about her love for a man her father disapproved of.

That sounded familiar. Only Abby's father had been right. Who knew if Mother and her lover would've made a marriage work? They'd met in college, she the privileged daughter from a wealthy family, he a scholarship student from blue-color factory workers in Detroit. They met secretly for fear their relationship be reported to her family.

When his father died, he'd gone home to take care of the family, promising to keep in touch. She wrote to him about her pregnancy, the letter that went astray.

Abby didn't want to believe the truth in front of her. The last letter, the one in which he asked her to leave her husband and bring their daughter to him. They would be a family, he wrote. He would support them.

Since her mother never divorced her father, she knew the answer.

Abby stared at the letter's date. She would've been four months old. She was the baby. In that final letter, he'd signed his usual heart plus his name.

George.

CHAPTER ELEVEN

"Abby, dear. Aren't you done up here yet?" Mother called from the bottom of the stairs.

Numb, Abby continued to sit, the letter on her lap.

"Abby?" Mother trudged up the stairs. "What are you—"

"You should have told me, Mother." With a listless wave, she held up the letter.

Mother froze. For several moments, her mouth worked but no words came out. Finally, in a clipped voice, she said, "I told you not to read anything from that box. I said I wanted it burned. You promised not to read anything in there."

For several moments, Abby didn't speak. She held out the letter then said, "Is George Watson my father?"

Mother stiffened. "Your father is the man who raised you, the man who came to your dance recitals and your band concerts. Harold Ten Eyck's name is on your birth certificate. Harold Ten Eyck was your father."

"Let me rephrase that. Is George Watson my biological father?"

After a long pause, Mother nodded. With slow steps, she went downstairs.

Abby gathered the letters and put them into the new box, then followed.

Mother stood at the stove, the teakettle in her hand. She seemed lost in thought with an expression Abby had never seen before. Misery. Not even at her Father's—Harold's—funeral had she looked that way.

"Mother?"

Without looking at Abby, she turned on the stove then gathered two cups and saucers from the kitchen table and took them into the dining room. Back in the kitchen, Abby looked for a teapot and a box of teabags. She found them on the sideboard in the dining room then took them back to the stove.

Again, Mother stood off to the side deep in thought. Conflicting emotions crossed her face. Despair, joy, anguish, hope. Back to misery.

Abby prepared the tea and brought the pot to the dining room. "Please sit, Mom. We have a lot to talk about."

Without waiting, Abby sat. She lifted the teapot lid, checked the liquid, then dunked the bags up and down a couple of times to hurry the steeping process. Her mother finally sat. No, she slumped into a chair.

"I never wanted you to know."

"Why? It's my life."

"I didn't want you to know I was . . . promiscuous."

With a calmness she didn't feel, Abby poured the tea into each cup. "Were you? I mean, were you with other men?"

She snapped her head up. "Of course not. Only with George."

"Then I'd hardly call that being promiscuous." Abby took a slow sip of the hot tea. "Why did you marry Fath—Harold?"

"You can still call him Father." She fiddled with her spoon. "Our families wanted us to marry. I dated him a few times but never felt for him the way I did with George. Harold persisted even after I refused to marry him. Then I discovered I was pregnant with you." She smiled at Abby. "I was so thrilled. I called the number George had given me. A woman answered. I thought . . . I thought . . . I didn't know what to think. Still, I left my name and asked him to call. He didn't. I wrote to him, telling him about you. He never answered. I found out recently his older sister, worried that he'd leave them—leave her—to come here, never told him about my call. She hid my letter. Eventually, he found it and called. He said Harold had answered and told him we'd married. That's when George wrote that last letter."

"A calamity of selfish people." Abby scoffed. "I still don't understand why you married him."

"When I didn't hear from George, and Harold was still trying to get me to consider him, I told him the truth. That I was pregnant and, as I thought at the time, abandoned by the father. He agreed to marry me if I never told you, or anyone, the truth."

"So, he knew I wasn't his child?" That explained a lot of things—Father's aloofness, his demands for her to be the *perfect* child.

"Oh, yes. For years, he watched me to make sure I stayed faithful." She snorted. "As if I wouldn't be. I honored my vows. I put all thoughts of George aside."

"Yet, you kept his letters and your journals."

"I did. I knew that was wrong. In fact, until I saw that box after Thanksgiving, I'd forgotten about it. I suppose I should have burned all those letters before you were born."

Abby reached over and covered her mother's hand. "I'm glad you didn't. When I was growing up, I never thought you and Father had that close a relationship. I mean you two were married, but I never saw you sneak kisses—like Lexie's mom and dad did. Or Dottie's parents." She laughed. "Lexie, I mean Alex, used to get embarrassed when her dad patted her mother's rear end."

"No. Harold wasn't that demonstrative. Still, he loved me, and I did my best to show that I loved him."

Abby thought about how happy her mother was with George, remembered how he'd dipped her over his arm under the mistletoe. Her father would never have done that. If anyone else had done it, he would have shown his disapproval at such unseemliness.

"Now you and George have a second chance."

Her mother smiled broadly, and her eyes lit with joy. "We do. I'm so blessed to have found him again."

"You never said how you reconnected."

"The internet. Facebook."

"You are on Facebook? Why didn't you tell me?"

"Because I knew you wouldn't approve."

A twinge of hurt arrowed into Abby's heart. "I don't think—"

"You disapproved of so much. My new car, my new haircut and dye job, my wardrobe, my—"

"I'm sorry, Mom." Misery swamped her. "I am truly sorry. I thought too many things were changing too fast. I don't like change."

"I know, dear. You like the status quo. I see so much of Harold in you. You were very much his child."

"I'm not sure if I like that." It made her feel as if she'd been too straight-laced, disapproving, not at all the person she thought she was.

"He was afraid you'd turn out like me, going off with the wrong man. That only made you dig in your heels and keep dating Kevin."

"Father was right about him, though. I guess I should've listened. At least, I try to be more accepting of Bethany's choices."

"I've been very proud of the way you raised her. She's sensible, cautious—at times—but with the sense of humor you seemed to have lost after you returned home."

"Hard to have a sense of humor after you've been betrayed." Abby felt the outside of the teapot. Still warm. She hovered the pot over her mother's cup. "More?"

Getting a nod, she poured tea into both their cups.

"Abby, dear, I'm so glad to see you lightening up lately." She took a sip of her tea. "You and Sam are—"

"Sam? Oh my God. He's my brother. How could you and George let us—" Abby's words came out too fast. Her tongue twisted over them as her mind went off in several directions at once. "That's incest. Why didn't you say something? Oh my God. Sam's older than me. George must have been married when you— Oh, Lord. How—"

Mother slammed her hand on the table. "Stop. Let me get a word in. Please."

Abby realized her mother had tried to interrupt her raving. She took a breath and slowly blew it out.

"That's better, dear. Now listen carefully. George was not married when we had our affair. Sam is George's wife's son from a previous marriage. When Sam was little, George adopted him. No incest. No worries about being brother and sister. Okay?"

Abby rubbed her forehead. "I feel like a fool for carrying on. Of course, you two would have broken us up if we were related. I should have thought of that. Does Sam know about being adopted?"

"Of course."

"Does he know about me? About me being George's biological daughter?"

"I don't know."

Abby finished sorting the attic. She'd thought about going over to George's condo then thought better of it. She was still processing all she'd learned that afternoon. Having her whole life turned upside down took its toll. When she arrived home, Bethany had already gone to work in Grand Rapids. In the quiet of the apartment, she couldn't sit still. Eating dinner didn't appeal. Her mother had tried to get her to stay, but Abby needed space. Reading didn't help, either. She switched on the television then promptly switched it off. Nothing but reruns. And bad news.

Unlike her mother, Abby enjoyed leaving the Christmas decorations up after New Year's. Now it was time to put it all away. Gathering up the decorations went quickly. It took longer to find the boxes in the storage area. When she finished, her home looked bare. Not at all festive as it had been for weeks. She had to replace the pictures and decorations that normally added color to the living room. Instead, she sat in her stuffed chair and contemplated what she'd learned that day.

The buzzer sounded. The last thing she wanted was company. Bethany had taken the van to work, so no one would know she was there. The buzzer went off again. Again, she ignored it.

Her cell phone vibrated on the table next to the chair. She expected the caller to be her mother.

Unknown caller. Not the local area code. Probably a robo-call. Bad enough they deluged the landline. Somehow, they'd gotten her cell number, too. Well, they could leave a message. She'd rather think about the man she'd always called Father. So much made sense. No wonder his approval had been hard to achieve. Would she have acted differently if she'd known? At least, she wouldn't have banged her head against a wall to get what was never forthcoming.

Her phone pinged that she had a voice mail message.

It would keep pinging until she looked. With exasperation, she listened.

George. He was outside in his car, waiting until she came home. She couldn't leave him out there, in the cold and dark. She called him back.

He slowly trudged up the stairs as she stood in the doorway. The usual lightness in his step missing.

When he looked up, he stopped. "Abby."

She stepped aside to let him in. "George. Can I take your coat?"

He hesitated. "Sure."

After she hung up his coat and scarf, she invited him into the living room and turned on the overhead light.

"You were sitting in the dark?" he asked.

"Not exactly." She nodded at the soft light from the lamp next to her chair.

He settled into her chair, leaving the couch for her.

"Can I get you something to drink?"

He shook his head. "I'm sure you have questions."

She shrugged then leaned back and put her sock-clad feet on the coffee table.

George cleared his throat. "I thought about you all the time. Your mother never talked to me after you— I mean, I never knew when you were born, so

I guessed the date. I celebrated your birthday every year. I bought you gifts. I wanted to send them to you, but my dear wife reminded me that you had a father. Besides, I had no idea where you lived. So, I packed the gifts in a box and kept them, thinking when I saw you I could give them to you."

"Did your wife resent that you spent money on a child you would never see?"

"Actually, she encouraged me. Sam knew I had another child. He knew I couldn't see you. That you had a family. I never told him your name because I didn't know it. Not until I met Flo again."

"He knows now?"

George shook his head. "I had to wait for Flo. And I wanted to talk to you first. I would never have abandoned Flo. God gave us a second chance. I'm going to do my damnedest to make up for lost time. I'd like to do the same with you."

"I'm not sure you can. With either of us. What's past is past. We can only go forward. I want my mother to be happy. Bethany keeps reminding me that Mother is different with you. More carefree, laughing often. She is genuinely happy." She paused. "She was never like that with Fath—with Harold."

"You can and should call him Father. He was your father in all the ways that count. I will admit to feeling jealous that he was there for all your firsts, and that I wasn't." He slowly got to his feet, using the chair arms to lever himself up. "I'm sorry I wasn't there for you or your mother."

She rose, too. "But you're here now. Isn't that what's important?"

Since he seemed hesitant, she stepped forward to give him a hug. Tears gathered in his light blue eyes. He moved away and, surreptitiously, swiped at his dampened cheeks.

"I am glad you know." His voice sounded clogged with tears. He quickly left.

Abby locked the apartment door behind him then leaned back against it. *Now what did she do?*

Was her mother right in not telling her about her origins? If she had gotten pregnant out of wedlock, would she have told Bethany? When?

A pounding on the door behind her, startled Abby. *Who could have come up the stairs without her buzzing them in?*

"Abby?" Sam demanded through the heavy fire door. "Let me in."

She jerked the door open. "What—"

"What did you say to my father?" His gray eyes resembled storm clouds over Lake Michigan.

"Hello to you, too." She backed away.

He grabbed her arm. "I met my father as he was leaving here. Why is crying? He's out there in the dark, in his car, bawling his eyes out. What did you say to him? I know you don't like your mother dating him, but—"

"Who said I don't like them dating?" She yanked her arm away from his grip and fisted her hands on her hips. She'd had one hell of a day and now this guy—this guy she thought was different— was acting like she was to blame for George's misery.

Sam scraped his hand down his face. "Oh, for God's sake. Just tell me what you said to him. The only time I ever saw my dad cry was when we lost Mom."

"Did you ask him?" She wasn't sure she should be the one to tell Sam about what she'd just learned.

"Of course, I did. He said to ask you or wait until I got home."

Oh, great. Lay it on me. Thanks, George.

"You might as well take off your coat. This may take a while." She went into the kitchen. "Do you want something to drink?"

She heard the rattle of the heavy metal hangers used for coats in the front closet, but no answer on drinks. She needed something stronger than water or pop. After grabbing a can of ginger ale out of the fridge, she opened the cupboard above it where she kept liquor. Standing on her tiptoes allowed her to reach the bottle of Canadian Club with her fingertips.

Sam hip-bumped her out of the way and brought down the bottle. "That good, huh?"

"Oh, yeah." She splashed a good shot of CC into her glass, added ice, then the Vernor's. "What can I get you? I know you don't drink liquor."

"Am I going to need it?"

"Maybe. Fix what you want." She left him standing in the kitchen and curled up in the corner of the couch.

He returned with a glass filled with ice and something amber. Ginger ale or Canadian Club? After settling in the chair George had just vacated, he waited.

"I wish to God our parents had told us everything." She took a long swallow of the mixed drink. "Hang onto your hat, kid. Are you ready for this? Your father is my father."

Sam sputtered and choked on his drink. He yanked a handkerchief out of his pocket and wiped his mouth. "So. You're the one."

"What? You know?"

"Yes. That my dad had a child. Not that you were her. I didn't expect such a blunt announcement."

"Sorry. I guess I should have eased into it. Not that there was much easing when I learned."

"Tell me." That sounded less like an order, more like plea.

She took a deep breath. "I was cleaning out the attic, looking for stuff to save and/or throw away." She told him about finding the box after Thanksgiving and her mother's dictate that she burn the contents after she was gone. Without reading.

"Are you going to get to the point soon?"

"Be patient, damn it. I'm still trying to wrap my head around the fact that your father and my mother had an affair, and I'm the result."

Sam nodded. "When did you find out?"

"This afternoon. The box broke, letters scattered. I read the letter on top. And read more. Freaked. Mother found me reading. She freaked. She told me what happened. I freaked more thinking we were sister and brother. I didn't know he wasn't your real father."

"George *is* my real father." Sam paused to take a drink. "My biological dad died in a car accident when I was four. Mom married George a couple of years later. He was always there for me, a real father."

"You always knew then. No big shocker. My mother chose to keep it all a secret. Her affair, my biological father. She thought I would be ashamed of her promiscuity, as she called it. She should have told me."

"If that's what she believed, I can see why she didn't. Not when you were young, anyway. And not as a teen. She would think her story would give you *ideas*." His mouth quirked in a wry grin. "But when should she have?"

"I keep asking myself that. After Father died? When she reunited with George? Was there ever a good time? Maybe when the boys brought down the box before Christmas. Perfect timing there."

"Wasn't that around the time she told you she was selling the house? Maybe she thought it was too much for you to take in."

"Do not side with her."

Sam held up his hands. "Hey, I'm not the bad guy here."

"I know." She stretched out her legs, propped her feet on the coffee table, and crossed her arms. "I'm having a hard time accepting all the changes. Mother and George dating. The house being sold. And then finally figuring out why my father—why Harold—was always so standoffish. I was an unpleasant reminder that she'd had a lover before him. No wonder I could never measure up to his standards of perfection."

Without warning, tears began streaming down her face. She swiped them away with the back of her hand, but more kept coming.

Sam shot off the chair and sat beside her. He pulled her close and let her bawl as he muttered nonsense into her hair.

Bethany found them there when she came in from work.

"What did you do to my mother?"

Sam heard his own words and attitude reflected in Bethany's voice. He deserved it. He'd come down on Abby with hobnail boots over George's tears. Now, Abby's daughter turned the tables on him.

Abby straightened then rubbed her eyes. "It's not Sam's fault. Don't yell at him."

Still wearing her coat, hat, and scarf, Bethany plopped in the chair and propped her elbows on the arms. "I'm waiting."

"Not now, sweetie. I'll tell you later."

"Uh uh." She crossed her legs. "Tell me now."

"I should leave." Sam started to rise, but Abby tugged on his arm to sit. "Or not." He shrugged.

While Abby gave a brief explanation, Bethany sat in stunned silence.

"I know it's a lot to take in, sweetie. I'm not handling this well."

Still holding her close, Sam clasped her hand. "George always loved you, even though he didn't know your name. We had a birthday party ever year on what he thought was your birthday. Mom even made a cake for you, just like she did for me."

Abby smiled. "She did? I mean, he told me about the gifts. I didn't know about a party and cake."

"The party was Mom's idea, Besides your birthday, you got gifts every Christmas and Easter. I ate your candy, though." He grinned. "Dad called you his precious daughter. He always hoped that Flo would let him know about you."

"Do you still have the presents?" Bethany asked as she shed her winter garments.

"No. For a long time, Dad kept them in a box in our basement storage room. When you would've turned eighteen, Mom suggested we give the gifts to the kids at the hospital. Dad felt like we were giving up, but he finally understood the reasoning, especially when he saw those kids' eyes light up."

"That was generous of him," Abby said.

"My point was that he thought of you often. Sometimes, I was jealous of my phantom sister. As a kid, I wanted all his attention. As an adult, I admired how he handled missing you. But I would've done more to find you. Hired a detective, even."

"Like Alex O'Hara," Bethany said. "She's a private investigator and my mom's friend."

Abby looked at him and smiled. "He knows Alex."

"Is that why you were crying when I came in?"

"It's all so overwhelming." She twisted the handkerchief he'd given her. "Everything I thought about myself isn't true. I'm not who I thought I was."

Sam shifted then clasped her shoulders. "You are still the same person, Abigail Louise Ten Eyck. It's your perception that's changed."

She pulled away. "Why do you have to be so damn reasonable?"

"Mo-ther, language," Bethany exclaimed with false indignation. "Besides, he's trying to help."

Abby grimaced. She tried so hard not to cuss in front of her daughter. "Sam, do you mind? I need some time alone."

He leaned over and kissed her forehead. "Dad and I have a lot to talk about." He straightened. "I'm glad we're not true brother and sister.

She gave him a small smile. "Me, too."

CHAPTER TWELVE

The next evening, they gathered at her mother's. Abby wished they hadn't waited so long to get together, but she couldn't leave her store until then. George gave her a strong hug. When he hugged Bethany, he said, "I always wanted a granddaughter. I thought by marrying your grandmother, I'd finally get my wish. Now, I find out I've had one all along."

Bethany looked pleased, and her mother smiled broadly. Sam looked deep in thought. When they entered, he'd given Abby a distracted kiss. She wondered what was going on in his head. But then her mother announced she'd gotten through the entire first floor deciding what to keep and what to leave, and Abby was distracted as well.

After a modest dinner, a chicken casserole and a salad, they sat around the dining room table still talking about the wonders of second chances. At least, that's what George and Mother talked about.

"You're awfully quiet, Sam" his father said.

He stretched back in his chair before reaching down to clasp Abby's hand. "I guess this is as good a time as any. Since Flo is moving in with Dad, I'm moving out."

Abby's heart sank. *He's leaving.* She'd known he would. What man would settle in tiny Far Haven after living in the Big Apple. He had to be restless. He'd said he didn't want to go back to New York. That left a lot of big cities. Chicago, Houston, Los Angeles.

She tried to slide her hand out of his, but he squeezed her fingers.

"You're moving out?" Flo cried. "Please don't on my account."

"Where will you go?" Bethany asked.

Abby watched Sam's gaze go from Mother to George to Bethany, then land on her. "I bought a house."

This time her heart squeezed tighter than he squeezed her fingers.

She could hardly breathe. "Where?"

"Here." He stared deep into her eyes.

"Here in Far Haven?" Bethany asked. "I'm so glad."

"No. Yes, Far Haven. But I meant here. This house."

"What?"

"No."

"You what?"

Voices clamored, all asking the questions that roared through Abby's head.

Sam knocked on the table. "May I speak?" His mouth quirked. "I bought your house, Flo. I'm sorry for the subterfuge. I wanted it to be a done deal before revealing that I was your mysterious buyer. I wanted to keep everything on a professional level, no sentimentality. But with all the tears and heartache I've been seeing tonight, I knew I had to tell you."

Mother rushed around the table. She put her arms around Sam's neck and kissed his cheek. "Thank you." She stood behind him for several seconds. "I wanted to give Abby the house. I wanted it to stay with the family. I would've given her the money for the taxes, and so on. But I know my Abby. Pride wouldn't let her accept."

"That's right," she agreed. "I wouldn't."

"Pride, Mom?" Bethany asked.

Mother glared at them then cleared her throat for attention. "My plan is to give some of the proceeds from the house to you, Bethie, for college, so you can go wherever you want. Abby, I'm paying off your loan. No arguing."

Abby gaped at her mother. So did Bethany. Speechless. Both of them.

"I'm buying a smaller house up on the bluff south of town. Besides a great view of Lake Michigan, it has tall ceilings for some of my big furniture, like the secretary."

Now George gaped at her. "B-But I thought you were moving in with me?"

She walked around to his chair, clasping the back. "I love you, George Watson, but your condo is too small for me."

He reached behind him, covering her hand. "We will talk. Later." He smiled before turning his attention on Sam. "Your generosity makes me so proud of you, son. But you don't need to buy Flo's house. Looks like my condo is available." He chuckled.

"Thanks, Dad. No offense, but I don't want your condo. I want this place."

"Why?" Abby had to clear her throat. "I won't marry you just so I can keep this house in the family."

"Have I asked you to marry me?"

Abby's cheeks burned in embarrassment. *That'll teach me not to jump to conclusions.*

"Abby, when I do ask you to marry me, it will be because I love you and know that you love me in return."

She pulled her hand out of his clasp and buried her head in her arm on the table.

"What's going on?" Trust Bethany to cut to the chase. "I'm so confused."

"You don't have to buy this house out of charity," Abby's mother said.

"No charity, Flo. I love this place. I've never felt more at home since Mom died. I feel the love of generations here. It's perfect for a family, which I hope to have." He glanced at Abby, who'd looked up while he was talking.

"Besides," he went on. "The garage is perfect for my work."

He and George chuckled.

"You bought this house for the workshop?" Abby asked.

"Weren't you listening, Mom? He did it because he knows how much you love the place. He wants to marry you and have a bunch of kids."

While Abby gaped at her, Sam grinned. "When did you get to be so smart?"

Bethany straightened in her chair. "I come from a long line of Ten Eyck women. If Mom is as smart as the rest of us, she'll say yes when you pop the question."

Happy to be out of the house and alone with Sam, Abby strolled down the sidewalk, their gloved fingers entwined. So, he was the mystery buyer. She had a hard time wrapping her mind around that. Sam actually bought her family home.

"You want a bunch of kids, huh?"

His answer was a squeeze of her fingers. For several moments, she wondered if he was going to say more. When he didn't, she said, "I'm thirty-seven years old. If you want many children, you'll need to find a younger woman."

He led her across the street to the small city park. As the wind off the lake picked up, the swings danced, chains twisting. In the shade of a large maple, he stopped. After stripping off his gloves and tucking them into his jacket pockets, he framed her face with his warm hands.

"I do want to have children. The number is inconsequential. Their mother is most important. I want you to be the mother of my children. Your age isn't an issue. I'm no spring chicken myself." With a grin, he slid his hands down her shoulders to her hands. Sobering quickly, he clasped her hands as he knelt. "Abigail Louise, I love you. Will you marry me?"

Abby's heart thudded louder than the drumline in the high school marching band.

"Samuel George, I love you. More than you'll ever know. Of course, I'll marry you."

Thank you for reading **Romance Rekindled**. I hope you enjoyed my story. It would be great if you let others know. Authors love reviews. If you have time, please consider leaving a review at Goodreads and/or your online retailer — even just a line or two about what you thought of the book would be so appreciated.

P.S. You can read more about Abby and Sam, Florence and George in *The Case of the Meddling Mama (An Alex O'Hara Novel)*

Turn the page for a quick look at

*The Case of the Bygone Brother:
An Alex O'Hara Novel*

by Diane Burton

An Excerpt from **_The Case of the Bygone Brother_**
(the first Alex O'Hara novel)

CHAPTER 1

She had trouble written all over her.

Like a scene out of _The Maltese Falcon_, a beautiful woman begs the PI for help. Shades of Sam Spade, with a slight difference. The elegantly-dressed woman pounding on my plate glass window was more than twenty years older than me and, even though my name is Alex O'Hara, I'm not male. But I am a PI —O'Hara & Palzetti, Confidential Investigations since 1965. Not that I've been around since 1965.

I started working for The Pops—Frank O'Hara and Tony Palzetti—in my teens as a go-fer. After seeing how women in the business were treated, I reinvented myself by shortening my name from Alexandra to Alex. Having what could be a man's name meant I wasn't immediately dismissed just because I'm a woman.

As if being on my own wasn't hard enough since The Pops retired, some people consider private investigating a man's job. Thank God, The Pops weren't narrow-minded. Lots of women are investigators. I met many of them at conferences. It's just that the general public thinks digging up dirt on people or raking through their trash is a sleazy occupation, not fit for women. It's a different story when _they_ want to hire us to dig and rake.

Despite the late hour on a Friday evening, lights blazed in the reception area and my inner office door stood partially open. She could tell someone was home. At first, she tapped delicately, fingernails on glass. That sound barely registered since I was up to my eyeballs trying to figure out how I could pay my receptionist, the utilities, my loan to The Pops, and still eat. Ramen noodles would be making a comeback in my diet.

When she rapped with her knuckles, I finally glanced up—through the hunk of red hair that had escaped the scrunchie at the back of my head. My hairdresser calls my hair auburn. But auburn better described Mom's beautiful hair. Mine's just plain red.

The woman cupped her hands and peered through the window. She caught my eye and beckoned. As I rounded my desk, I reattached the scrunchie, unrolled the long sleeves of my white blouse and tucked it into my black slacks. I closed the door to get the matching jacket hung on the back. That's when she resorted to pounding on the outer door. Maybe she thought I was hiding. As if.

"All right, already," I muttered before abandoning the jacket and calling out, "I'm coming."

When I got a good look at her, I saw the answer to my budget problems. Money, not trouble, was scrawled all over her, from the top of her blonde, perfectly-coifed hair to the tips of her Manolo Blahnik's. In between, she wore a black Donna Karan sweater and skirt that cost more than I make in a week, or maybe a month. Add to that the Lincoln MKS parked in front of my office and you get my drift.

Wow. We don't see wealth like that in Far Haven, unless it's summer when our population triples with tourists who flock to the Lake Michigan beaches.

You're probably wondering how a small town private investigator who's barely making ends meet recognized Manolo and Donna. One of my dearest friends owns an exclusive dress shop in Grand Rapids. She lets me try on the merchandise and I get to pretend I'm one of the beautiful people. Go ahead, laugh.

As soon as I unlocked the outer door, the woman burst through, a few maple leaves stuck to her Manolo's. Frankly, I was surprised she wore only a sweater. She must have been freezing out there. In spite of the fact that it was mid-October, the temp had dipped that afternoon into the low forties. We might even get frost.

"Ms. O'Hara, thank God you're still here. I was so afraid—" She broke off on a sob. Taking a small, white, lace-edged handkerchief out of her Louis Vitton purse, she dabbed at her eyes.

Now I'm not one to belittle a person's worries. However, I thought she switched a little too quickly from imperious knocking to damsel in distress.

Damsel? Not quite. I pegged her around fifty-five, give or take a few years, and well-preserved. Even in her Manolo's, she only came up to my chin. Next to her I felt like a hulking giant. Since I'm five-ten in my socks, I look down on most women. Despite her elaborate up-do, from my angle I could see her roots. A visit to her hairdresser might be in order. But I digress.

"What can I do for you?" I tried not to sneeze from her overpowering perfume. An oriental scent. Shalimar or Opium. I never knew which was which. I tried them on at the perfume counter at Macy's. That's the closest I'd ever get to wearing expensive perfumes.

"I need your help." Her breathy voice reminded me of Marilyn. As in Monroe, not Manson.

Because Pop loved old movies, I became addicted to them. Just like I did with detective novels. I cut my teeth on Nancy Drew, moved on to the likes of Daphne duMaurier and P.D. James before graduating to Dashiell Hammett and Raymond Chandler. I watched *Masterpiece Mystery* on PBS and every movie Alfred Hitchcock made. In my teens, I watched reruns of *Remington Steele*. Once, I wore a fedora like Laura's to work. The Pops laughed so hard I never did again.

I ushered the woman into my office with its mahogany paneling and closed the door. I held out my hand. "As you've guessed, I'm Alex O'Hara." I looked at her expectantly.

She laid her hand in mine. I clasped hers firmly enough to reassure but gently enough not to crush the delicate bones beneath the cold skin.

"My name is Babette Rhodes. Babette Anslyn Rhodes."

She perched on the visitor's chair, her back finishing-school straight and knees pressed together. I took my place behind the desk in the big leather chair that had been Pop's. While she twisted the handkerchief, I stacked the bookkeeping papers and tucked them into the top desk drawer. Once I placed a clean legal pad in front of me, I folded my hands on top ready for her story. A story that could solve my financial problems.

"Ms. O'Hara, I must ask you to keep what I am about to tell you in absolute confidence."

"Of course." Hadn't she seen the word *confidential* on the sign on the door?

"My brother is missing. I must find him."

There went the anticipated influx to my revenue stream. "Missing persons is a police matter. Have you reported this?"

She waved the damp handkerchief. "I can't."

Her eyes welled up and she dabbed under them, managing not to smear her mascara. I'd only seen eyes that color once before. Elizabeth Taylor's. Such a soft violet. Unreal. Contacts?

"Why not?" I asked.

"It's been too long. Nearly ten years. And I'm not entirely sure he's missing. I—I just can't find him."

Okay, maybe not a loss. Hope began to grow.

"Perhaps you should start at the beginning," I suggested.

"We used to be close." She sniffled. "As close as siblings who live far apart. He always called on my birthday, no matter where he was. And we always got together at Mother's for Christmas."

When she dabbed at her eyes again, I reached behind me for the tissues I kept on the bookcase and pushed the box closer to her. She looked up and gave me a grateful smile before plucking a tissue. After putting away her now-sodden handkerchief, she continued to look at her closed purse while she talked.

"Mother died ten years ago. Since I lived close to her and Harry—well, his job kept him on the road a lot—I had to settle Mother's estate. Harry was not happy with the settlement. Never mind the reasons." She fluttered her hand. "He said . . . hurtful things. I, uh, responded in kind." She looked up at me. "I am not proud of that, Ms. O'Hara."

I nodded. Nothing split a family like a parent's estate. I'd seen it over and over.

"We haven't seen each other or even spoken since. I tried to stay in touch, sending cards, but they came back when he moved without a forwarding address."

After waiting for her to continue, I finally said, "You said ten years. Why now? Has something happened?" *And why come pounding on my door late on a Friday as if this were an emergency?*

"What they say about you is true, Ms. O'Hara. You really are perceptive."

Though pleased that others—no idea who—spoke well of me, I kept my expression neutral. Never gloat in front of a potential client.

"I—I'm sick."

She looked in good health. Still, who knew?

Giving me a weak smile, she said, "It's made me rethink my priorities. I want to reconcile with my brother. I—I don't want to wait any longer."

"All right, Ms. Rhodes. Let me get as much information about your brother as you know. His name is Harry, right?"

As she related what she knew, I wrote quickly. I got places and dates where he'd lived, especially his last known residence. Interestingly, the family used to live in Holland, the resort and college town just south of Far Haven.

"He always talked about retiring there."

"There are good investigators in Holland. Why come to me?"

"As I mentioned, I have heard good things about you. And . . . you're a woman. I knew you would understand. I am prepared to pay for your services." She mentioned an obscene amount of money.

I clenched my teeth, so my mouth didn't fall open.

"Will that be satisfactory?" she asked.

What was I supposed to say—no? My folks didn't raise a fool.

She opened her purse and pulled out an envelope, which she handed over. I looked inside. A whole lot of Benjamins looked back.

"I hope that will be all right for a retainer." She gave me such an expectant look I could only nod.

All right? Holy shit—sorry, Mom—the retainer alone could pay my bills for a couple of months.

"I will give you a receipt." I pulled the book out of my desk.

She waved that away. "That's not necessary. I trust you."

Nevertheless, I wrote it out. Pop always said the IRS liked to see receipts. But, holy Maltese Falcon, I've never written that many zeroes on a receipt before.

"Ms. Rhodes, I will do my best to find your brother." I handed over the receipt.

"I'm sure you will, dear."

"One more thing." I gave her my standard info form.

She glanced at it. "What is this?"

"Basic information."

"But I told you all I know about Harry." She did not look pleased.

"Yes, ma'am. I just need some information about you."

"Me? Whatever for?"

"Ms. Rhodes, I need your phone number where I can reach you and—"

She gave me a sharp look. "Why?"

That took me aback. "To let you know what I find. Or to ask more questions."

"Of course. I'm sorry. I'm staying with friends and I don't know their number. I'll have to call you."

"Your cell number will be fine."

She laughed. "Silly me. I never use that phone. I forgot all about it." She took it out of her purse. "I never know the number." She pressed a few screens then recited it.

I pointed to a line on the form. "Just write it down there. And then your address on the line below."

"My address?"

I tried hard not to roll my eyes. Was this dame ditsy or what? "Yes, ma'am. Your home address so I know where to send my report."

"I'll be staying in Grand Rapids until you find my brother."

"Then you're not from West Michigan?"

Again, she eyed me with suspicion. "I said I was only staying here until you find Harry."

"Then please write down both your home address and where you're staying."

She squinted at the paper. "Here? I don't have my glasses with me. I detest wearing them." After giving me a self-deprecating smile, she filled in the info.

I recited my standard policies then pointed to the bottom of the paper. "Please sign here, acknowledging that you agree."

"Is all this really necessary?"

"Yes, ma'am."

"I didn't realize hiring an investigator would be so . . ." She waved her hand. "I feel like *I'm* being investigated."

She looked ready to take back the envelope. The one with Ben Franklin and his clones inside. "I'm sorry you feel that way, Ms. Rhodes. It certainly wasn't my intention."

"If I must, I must." She scribbled her name. "Do you have any more questions for me?" Despite her smile, she sounded a bit peeved.

Well, pardon me. I wouldn't ask questions if I didn't need the answers. I took a deep breath to rein in my Irish temper. I may have inherited Mom's hair, but my blue eyes and temper came from Pop.

"I have to caution you, Ms. Rhodes, after ten years, it may be . . . difficult." I didn't want to say impossible. No sense talking about failure before even starting. However, the client needed to know that miracles were not part of my repertoire.

She rose. "I am certain you will use every resource you have at your disposal." She sniffed and dabbed before walking out. At the outer door, she turned. "Thank you, Ms. O'Hara. Reconciling with Harry is my dearest wish."

Holy Sam Spade. I watched her slide into her luxury car and drive off. This case was like a Dashiell Hammett book. Babette Rhodes might have had better luck with a male detective, given all the tears. But I certainly wasn't turning her down.

With a little skip, I locked the envelope with the money in the safe behind my favorite picture of the Mackinac Bridge then locked my desk, turned out the lights, and headed upstairs to my apartment. What a start to a great weekend.

Stories in the Far Haven world

The Case of the Begone Brother (An Alex
O'Hara Novel)

Romance Rekindled (A Far Haven Tale)

The Case of the Fabulous Fiancé (An Alex
O'Hara Novel)

The Case of the Meddling Mama (An Alex
O'Hara Novel)

About the Author

Diane Burton combines her love of mystery, adventure, science fiction and romance into writing romantic fiction. Besides the science fiction romance *Switched* and *Outer Rim* series, she writes romantic suspense and cozy mysteries (The Alex O'Hara Novels). She is also a contributor to to two anthologies, *How I Met My Husband* and *Portals, Volume 2*. Diane and her husband live in Michigan. They have two children and five grandchildren.

For more info and excerpts from her books, visit Diane's website: http://www.dianeburton.com

Connect with Diane Burton online

Blog: dianeburton.blogspot.com/
Facebook: Diane Burton Author
Twitter: @dmburton72
Pinterest: dmburton72
Goodreads: Diane Burton Author

If you would like to know when a new book is released, sign up for Diane's newsletter. http://eepurl.com/bdHtYf